DOCKET
No. 76

Arita M. L. Bohannan

authorHOUSE®

AuthorHouse™ LLC
1663 Liberty Drive
Bloomington, IN 47403
www.authorhouse.com
Phone: 1-800-839-8640

Published by AuthorHouse 01/23/2014

ISBN: 978-1-4918-5544-7 (sc)
ISBN: 978-1-4918-5543-0 (hc)
ISBN: 978-1-4918-5542-3 (e)

Library of Congress Control Number: 2014901132

This book is dedicated to the little girls and boys who live inside every abused adult and who is searching for an innocence that he or she must learn to live without. It is also dedicated to those parents who, through gentle and trustworthy love, guide those children to adulthood and help them become true and strong survivors rather than victims.

"For a lawyer to do less than his utmost is, I strongly feel, a betrayal of his client. Though in criminal trials one tends to focus on the defense attorney and his client the accused, the prosecutor is also a lawyer, and he too has a client: the People. And the People are equally entitled to their day in court, to a fair and impartial trial, and to justice."[1]

—Vincent Bugliosi

---

1   Bugliosi, Vincent. *Helter Skelter: The True Story of the Manson Murders* (New York: W. W. Norton and Company, 2001).

ACKNOWLEDGMENTS

FIRST, I WISH TO THANK MY PREVIEW PANEL. LISA, TONI, CHERYL, and Caitlyn, I thank you for having the guts to be honest with me! You loved me enough to risk hurting my feelings, and I will forever appreciate you for that.

I would like to acknowledge my aunts, Sandra M. and Sheila M. As a child, I thought you were the smartest and strongest women I had ever met. As an adult, I am certain you are. You two have shaped much of what and who I am today and I will always be grateful.

I also acknowledge my family: Robby (my oldest and dearest friend), Uncle Bob (who always looks out for his girls), Peter Thomas, Anthony, Pete, Laurie, Jesse, Seth, Tyler, Dude, Lisa, Connor, Caitlyn, Uncle Louie, Aunt Cathy and Uncle Bobby, Aunt Pat, Evelyn, Sunny, Linda, Jaimie, Uncle Charlie, Uncle LJ and Aunt Melinda, Jamie, Dalton, Nick, Kenny, Katie, Eric and Candy, Billy 'RPaw' Bohannan, Lauren and my (literally) dozens of cousins on both sides of the family!

I also wish to acknowledge my sister, Ann and her husband, Tommy. You have been a huge source of support since I was two years and eleven months old. Thank you for trusting and loving me, my sister—my friend.

I also acknowledge my parents, SFC Peter Thomas Lipps and Roslyn Lipps. You two have never left my side. Thank you for expecting me to be all that I could be. Your love and kindness helped me defy odds that surprised all of us. Dad, you may find yourself portrayed as a character in this book, but just know that it's because you always protected me, even when you weren't sure that you had. I love you both, Mom and Dad.

I would like to acknowledge my sons, Deuce and Bryce. One day, you will understand that when you look into the eyes of your child, your whole world changes. Somehow, everything you were becomes far less important. For Dad and I, all we want is your happiness, your success, and your love—and, of course, to be there to witness it. That you are proud to have me as your mom means the world to me.

I would like to acknowledge my husband, Bradley S. Bohannan Sr. Thank you for never saying no to whatever dream I decide to chase. You have given me your name, many memories, two of the most prized children in the world, and my future. There is no mountain you wouldn't climb for me or the boys. You make me feel important, and that is invaluable. You are my John Wayne, and for that I love you.

CHAPTER 1

THERE ARE SOME JOURNEYS THAT YOU CHOOSE TO TAKE...AND THEN there are some journeys that choose to take you, even if you are unwilling to go along for the ride.

Adorina Dauzat, nickname Dori, was the five-year-old daughter of Harold and Laurie Dauzat, who were the owners of a small boutique hotel in the French Quarter, where they maintained the top floor as their private apartment—which they frequently inhabited on weekends. The family's primary residence was in a part of New Orleans called Uptown. There, they lived in a rather famous and historic home called Blackacre.

Uptown is a section of New Orleans on the Mississippi River's East Bank. In the nineteenth century, it was developed from plantation lands. The area earned its designation because it is just uptown from the historic French Quarter. United States citizens, joined by immigrants and including a sizable African American community, came to reside in this section of the city, as it has always been an ethnically, racially, and economically diverse area. The Dauzats, however, lived on the famous St. Charles Avenue, which, since the 1800s, has been known as Millionaire's Row. In the 1800s, becoming a millionaire was even more of a challenge than it is today.

Historians say that Blackacre was a safe house for the Underground Railroad. The home still bears its original white color from the 1800s.

The columns that rise to the second story of the home were hand-carved by masterful artisans and neatly held the third-floor balconies. A pebble carriage pass carves its way through soft and plush green grass along the side of the home, ending only at the doors of the carriage house. Although this is now a modern driveway with the latest expensive import parked gracefully on the gravel, the Dauzats were careful to leave the same gravel driveway and carriage doors so that at any moment the modern conveniences could be removed and the home could be restored to its original splendor. While the carriage house had long ago been used as a driveway and playhouse for Dori, it all remained intact, including the large, barn-style doors that opened outward, rather than upward as in a modern-day garage. It was an absolutely divine play area for one of the luckiest—and one of the wealthiest—children.

One could picture the flowing gowns of the wealthy ladies who once graced these still beautiful gardens. Yes, it was a beautiful antebellum home, and it stood out as remarkable even in this neighborhood of incredibly beautiful homes.

The home to which the police were called that evening, however, was the residence of longtime family friend, Lee Lawson, who lived several streets away but within walking distance—on Prytania Street. Mr. Lawson was very well-known in the area. He owned a local architectural firm and had worked on various large projects throughout the city, including museums and a children's theater. He was just as well-known for his philanthropic pledges, however; on a regular basis, he graced the pages of the social section of the local newspaper for hosting or attending some of the largest fund-raisers in New Orleans.

Mr. Lawson was easy to remember with his strawberry blond hair, tall stature, and quick wit. One rarely saw him without a charming grin playing across his face. He was usually the first in a room to laugh. In fact, as a young man nearly forty years old, he was listed as one of the city's top ten bachelors. Interestingly, one never heard him boast of this. He found the fact rather embarrassing. And although he was not married, he was hardly lonely. The love of a New Orleans beauty wasn't exactly unfamiliar to him. Still, no woman had managed to hold his interest long enough for him to propose marriage.

Lawson was extremely proud of his meek beginnings. He grew up in a poor urban area of Missouri, had worked two jobs to put himself through college, and had sold the last thing he owned to open his own business.

No one rushed to beat down the doors of the Lawson Architectural Firm when he first opened the office. Not one to wait around, Mr. Lawson began volunteering and donating his time to restoring a school. It was an old historic building in New Orleans. He spent hour after hour attending city council meetings, code enforcement debates, and so on. The recognition he received from this endeavor led to the growth of his previously strained company.

Mr. Lawson made hard work and success seem easy. He was smart, sensitive, and loyal. Harold Dauzat often teased him that he was successful because he was good-looking enough that the ladies coaxed their husbands into hiring him! Whatever the reasons for his success, he was well-known, well liked, and well respected in New Orleans.

When Detective Curtis arrived at the house, he found Mr. Lawson sitting in the living room. As the detective walked into the home, he was immediately impressed with the décor. Curtis, whose own apartment was clean but was lucky to have two matching lamps, didn't normally pay a whole lot of attention to décor, but even he took the time to note the impressiveness of that first room.

The living room, with its dark green walls and deep colors of mahogany wood, should have been dark. But instead, the room was warmly lit with several expensive-looking iron lamps. Although formal and heavy in many ways, the room was also comfortable and cozy.

Mr. Lawson was sitting in a large leather couch in front of the lit fireplace, holding a child in his lap. He was rocking back and forth. His arms fully encompassed the child, with her head resting on his shoulder, supported by the crease of his elbow, and her legs crossing his other arm. She appeared to be lying lifeless, except for her consistent deep sobbing. There were no fresh tears on her tearstained face—just this deep, internal sob. The child was wearing a white long nightgown that was partially bloodied and bunched up in areas. Her wrists appeared to have gray duct tape wrapped around them, although, clearly, it had been cut or torn in the middle so as to free each individual hand.

On Mr. Lawson's hands, arms, neck, and sweatpants were small spots and smears of blood. It was obvious from the bloody wipe marks across his face that he, too, had been crying. His eyes were frantic.

Mr. Lawson was arguing with the paramedics when Detective Curtis walked in. He could hear Mr. Lawson's raised voice as he approached the room. "You're going to need someone bigger than you to take her from me," Lawson was saying fiercely. His face was red, his eyes full of intense anger. The child's eyes were closed. She held onto Mr. Lawson, who continued to rock feverishly. Mr. Lawson's knuckles were white as they clenched together, his hands tightly holding the child close to his chest.

The paramedic, growing angry himself, tried again. "Look, sir. I'm just doing my job. You want us to help her, don't you?"

Mr. Lawson spat, "You're going to help her *my* way, asshole!"

Curtis quickly gathered that Mr. Lawson had insisted that he accompany the child to the hospital. He refused to let her out of his sight. The paramedic tried to ask Dori questions, but Mr. Lawson interrupted him, yelling, "Leave her alone. She's just a baby. Back off!"

Detective Curtis sat next to Mr. Lawson on the couch and tried to talk with him so as to defuse the situation. His tone was calm but firm. He put his hand on Lawson's shoulder. "Mr. Lawson, I can appreciate that you are upset."

Lawson yanked his head to look at Curtis. "I'm upset?! What are you? Some kind of prophet? Back the fuck away from us."

Curtis didn't move. "Look at her. It's obvious she is bleeding. Let us help her," he said coaxingly.

"No. I just … I don't … can't." Lawson shook his head feverishly.

"We don't know how bad this is, my friend. I want to help you, but I can't let that little lady suffer anymore. Do you understand, Mr. Lawson? She's hurting. She needs help. She's safe, but they need to take her."

Mr. Lawson sighed. He knew the detective was right. Within minutes, Detective Curtis had talked him into letting the paramedics take the child from his arms, but he had made Curtis promise that he would drive Mr. Lawson to the hospital himself.

Once Mr. Lawson had finally relented, he stood to place the child in the female paramedic's arms. As he did so, the child began to scream hysterically. She reached out her arms for him, a harsh, gurgling scream coming from deep inside her. There were no words, just the loud echo of her scream. She clung to his neck desperately. The paramedic firmly grabbed onto her and pulled quickly. Dori left scratch marks on Mr. Lawson's neck in her last attempt to stay put.

The paramedic quickly turned to carry the child out the door as Mr. Lawson reached to retrieve her. She was gone before he could stop the paramedic from taking her.

He turned to the detective and said, "Something almost killed her, and now I've broken her heart. She thinks I left her." His voice began to crack. "Let's go."

"One of the officers will drive you," Detective Curtis said. Mr. Lawson nodded, grabbed his keys, and walked out the front door. Curtis intentionally neglected to mention that they would stop at the police station. As Curtis and another officer put Mr. Lawson in the back of the police car, the detective looked at him, noting the pain on his face and the pure fear in his eyes.

"Take him to the station," the detective instructed the officer. "Put him in an interview room until I arrive."

All things considered, Mr. Lawson made a great suspect. He had been found alone with the child, he was an unmarried man, he wouldn't allow the child to talk to the paramedics or the police, and he was covered in blood. By all accounts, it appeared that the child had been injured at that location. Yes, Lawson made a nice suspect, all right.

Still, the way he had held the child, and the way the child had screamed for him, led the detective's gut feeling in a different direction. Something didn't sit right. Determined to understand what had happened at this residence tonight, Curtis set about collecting the evidence.

As he walked through the house, he noted that the entire home was immaculate. The dark wood trim, the masculine color scheme, and the exquisite décor made it clear that Mr. Lawson was in a lucrative industry. Detective Curtis thought to himself, *No, this guy isn't broke.* It hadn't appeared that the front door had been tampered with, and there were no signs of a struggle. The detective decided to begin his investigation upstairs, where he found four bedrooms.

As he approached the top of the staircase, he saw five doors, three of which were shut. One of these rooms was a large guest bathroom. Behind the two other doors were bedrooms, the lights therein turned off. The detective noted that the windows were shut and that both rooms appeared to have been unoccupied tonight.

The door directly in front of the detective, once he topped the stairs, was wide open. After peering in, Curtis assumed that this had been the bedroom the child had occupied. The bed was a large four-poster with a beautiful, gold-colored satin comforter and matching sheets. The furniture was oversized and appeared heavy and expensive.

It was not the typical bedroom furniture one would ordinarily expect to find in a child's room. In fact, the only indication of the child's presence was an open ballerina suitcase sitting on a chaise lounge, the baby doll lying in the middle of the bed, and a pink nightlight bearing a picture of a princess on it.

The blankets had been pulled down. The child's head had indented the pillow, where it appeared she had been resting peacefully at one time. Other than the fact that the sheets and blankets were slightly pulled back, there was nothing in the room to indicate any type of struggle. There was no blood on the sheets or on the floor. The lamp on the nightstand and the other furnishings did not appear to have been moved or knocked over. In fact, unless you had witnessed the horrific scene downstairs, you would think that the child had simply awakened in the night to use the potty.

At the end of the hall were two large double doors. Both stood wide open for the detective to enter the room. It was obvious upon his initial approach that this was Mr. Lawson's bedroom. The enormous bed sat opposite a large stone fireplace, inside of which was a nearly extinguished fire. On the bed, the blankets on the left-hand side nearest an adjoining bathroom had been pulled back. It appeared that this was where Mr. Lawson had been asleep. On the bed were a pair of small wire reading glasses and a book that had been turned upside down to mark a particular page. From the armoire, the glow and soft murmur of the local news from the television set seeped into the room.

This room, too, was immaculate, although notably more lived in. Besides the décor, which screamed "wealth" and "bachelor," the only other message the room conveyed is that Mr. Lawson had been resting peacefully and quietly herein. There was simply no evidence of a struggle. The detective stood at the foot of the bed, with one hand on his hip, confused. He had expected to see some type of smoking gun that would indicate that the wrongdoing had begun here, in Mr. Lawson's sanctuary. The windows in this room, as with all the upstairs rooms, were shut and locked.

Detective Curtis yelled down the stairs, "Crime lab, ASAP," indicating to the crime lab analyst that he was ready. A couple minutes later, a fellow officer dressed in blue cargo pants and a white shirt with "NOPD" on the back came bouncing up the stairs.

"Crosby—is that you?" He greeted the officer. Before Crosby could respond, Detective Curtis asked, "You no longer on the injury reserve list?" referring to a recent back injury Crosby had suffered.

Crosby seemed older than his fifty years. He was short, a little round, and balding. Still, he was great at his job—if you didn't mind staying on top of him a bit.

Crosby replied, "Yeah, doin' much better. Just needed a couple weeks to heal." Then he paused and, chuckling in anticipation of his own joke, said, "Either that, or I just got tired of having to spend time with my old lady!"

"Hey, spending time with the old lady is how you hurt your back in the first place!" replied Detective Curtis, laughing.

"Funny. Very funny," Crosby replied, with a "Like I haven't heard that one a hundred times" countenance. "All right, so where do you want me to start?"

Detective Curtis gave Crosby direction, specifying that he should look for any kind of child pornography. "Check his movies, his DVR, you know, just to make sure. Grab a copy of his hard drive, too."

"Grab a copy of his hard drive?" Crosby said sarcastically. He pulled out his phone and rolled his eyes while he dialed a number. "Just get a copy of his hard drive. Sure, no biggie." Then, with the phone to his ear, he said, "Hey, Tyndall, I need a hard drive copied. … No, now. Yes, right now. We are still at the scene, so grab your stuff." Then, turning back to Curtis, he smiled and said, "Consider it done."

Curtis nodded at him knowingly and turned to head downstairs.

As he rounded the bottom of the stairs, another officer grabbed his attention. "Detective, we found something in the kitchen."

Detective Curtis walked through the formal living room into a large kitchen. With dark granite countertops and marble flooring, the room certainly fit the rest of the home. *Gold faucets*, thought Curtis; *what a weirdo.*

The marble floor stretched beyond the kitchen and into the informal dining room, which featured a very heavy glass and wrought iron table and matching wrought iron chairs. Just past the table was a door at the back of the house. It stood open. The lights on the back patio were bright yellow and glowing.

"There it is, sir," said the officer, pointing at the entryway and the door.

And there it was. It was a single roll of gray duct tape, seemingly the exact same tape as had remained on one of the child's wrists when the detective had first arrived. The roll lay right near the door as if someone had dropped it on his or her way into the house. *Strange place to drop it*, thought Curtis. "Don't touch it," he said, staring at the tape and pondering the significance of its location. He paused before yelling over his shoulder, "Crime lab, ASAP!"

Also in the kitchen was a coffee cup, two bowls, and two spoons in the sink. Literally. Curtis thought that this was the cleanest kitchen he had ever seen. Even the refrigerator was organized. Leftovers had dates written on them. The detective thought of his own kitchen. His leftovers were still in the takeout boxes in which they had come, and several newspapers were strewn on the kitchen counter, which he used as a chair in the morning. He couldn't remember the last time he had washed his dishes.

"Detective," yelled an officer from outside, "out back."

Detective Curtis stepped out onto a small wooden deck that had two steps leading down to a large, open courtyard. Like the rest of the home, the courtyard was immaculately groomed. Large potted plants lined the small staircase and a short walkway, continuing into the courtyard. There was a large built-in grill to the far left, a large tree in the center of the courtyard, and several small tables and chairs circling the tree.

The yard was dimly lit by two antique wrought iron gas lanterns. A dark cherry wood fence provided the courtyard some privacy. Stepping down into the courtyard, Curtis noticed small, clear lights in the trees and plants alike. These reminded him of the Christmas lights used to light a yard during parties. The detective could almost hear faint laughter and the clinking of Champagne flûtes.

"Here it is, sir," said the officer.

Detective Curtis walked down the staircase and onto the side of the deck to search the spot the officer had indicated, his eyes searching the ground. The small area of grass was neatly trimmed. There was one small potted plant. One could see under the deck if one stooped, but the deck was too low for someone to hide beneath.

The area was quite dark because the back door light was high and the gas lanterns were far away. Even so, Curtis was able to see light reflecting off of what he estimated to be a six- to eight-inch strip of gray duct tape. He took a knee to get a better look when Crosby walked out.

"Whatta we got, Detective?" he asked, rubbing his lower back.

"I need to print this. Swab both sides for DNA. I need prints of the door, that table inside, and the tape on the table. I also want the counters, the front door, the banister." Half to himself, the detective said, "Hm. This would be easier if I was clear about the point of entry. Do you think you can get anything off this deck?" he asked.

"Nah, too porous. Can't ever get nothin' from wood," replied Crosby.

"Okay," sighed Curtis. "Did we get anything upstairs?"

"Bunch of prints," said Crosby, opening what looked like a tackle box and then taking from it strips of print tape and other tools of the trade. "Probably just the rich dude's and the kid's, though."

"You never know," said Curtis. His actual words seemed optimistic, although his tone of voice made it clear that he agreed with Crosby. He sighed again. "See you back at home base," said Curtis as he stood up and walked back into the house.

Curtis took another look around before making sure that the other crime scene officer had taken pictures of every inch of the home. Then he hopped into his unmarked car and headed back to the station to interview his only witness—who was also his only suspect.

CHAPTER 2

CURTIS STEPPED OFF THE ELEVATOR ONTO THE THIRD FLOOR. Two left turns later, he entered the child abuse unit of New Orleans Police Department (NOPD). It was a large, rectangular room with a couple of rows of standard-issue, outdated brown metal desks. His captain stood waiting at his desk, pacing angrily.

Captain Anthony Peters was a tall, slightly overweight, and usually serious man. In fact, *serious* was an understatement; *grumpy* was closer to the truth. He had a full head of gray hair. And although he was usually in a foul mood, he was quick to unload his anger on one officer and move onto the next, never holding a grudge. It was actually a good quality for a captain. One would go in, get his or her ass chewed out, and then move on—not having to worry that the captain would later carry on about the matter.

Skipping all niceties and not even bothering to say hello, the captain asked, "What the hell is going on here?" Without waiting for a response, he continued, his face reddening. "That's Lee Lawson!" he exclaimed, pointing in the general vicinity of the interview rooms. He paused, waiting to see some kind of response in Curtis's expression. Finding none, he repeated, "Lee Lawson," stressing the words and raising his eyebrows. "He's cuffed. And let's just say he's pissed to high heaven. Almost ripped the head off the rookie you sent him with. You better have something here."

"I didn't ask that he be cuffed, sir," replied Curtis, caught a bit off guard by the captain's attitude. "The kid was at his house. What was I supposed to do, send him a questionnaire?"

"Cute, Curtis, but it's my ass tomorrow when this hits the press." The captain began walking away. He stopped, turned on his heel to face Curtis, and pointed at him, saying authoritatively, "Get what you need, and then you let him go. Do you hear me? If you keep him, I want to know about it immediately—and let's just say that you better have probable cause pouring out of your ass, Curtis." The captain again turned on his heel and stormed out of the children's unit.

Great, thought Curtis, shaking his head in disbelief. *I have Captain Jackass up my tail, and now I get to spend the rest of my night with a likely child batterer.*

The detective's phone rang just at that moment. "Curtis," he answered, aggravated. He plopped into his rolling desk chair that may have been older than he was.

"Officer Tyler," said the voice on the other end. "I'm your reporting officer on this Dauzat kid."

"Yep, whatcha got?" asked Curtis as he rolled his chair to the little coffee table and poured himself a cup of cold coffee.

"Okay, so, the doc, uh, Doctor Leila Mayer, said it looks like she was raped. She did a kit on her. The kid needed stitches—you know, uh, in her female area." Tyler pause, bothered. "She's a real mess, Detective. Won't talk to anybody." Officer Tyler drew a deep breath before saying, "I think I'll hear that kid crying in my sleep." The officer paused. Detective Curtis tried to think of something to say to the young officer, who was obviously trying to get rid of a lump in his throat.

"Uh, yes. I know what you mean. It's a ... uh ... you know, it's a tough one. So, uh, yes." He searched for words. "By the way, did the parents show?"

Tyler replied, "Yes, sir. They got here a couple of minutes ago. They're all dressed up. The dad's wearing a leotard as part of his costume. Just seems strange in this setting, you know, a hospital and all. Anyhow, they are pretty tore up. Said that it doesn't make sense about their friend, uh"—Tyler paused as if reviewing his notes— "Lawson. Yeah, this guy Lawson. The dad said he's known him since they were kids and that he loves their daughter. He said it couldn't be him. The wife, though, Laurie Dauzat, said that this Lawson guy was accused of rape in high school. They really seemed offended. I even asked them, you know, considering that their daughter was lying in a hospital bed."

"I see. Okay, thanks for that. Oh, and Tyler, don't forget to bag her clothing, underwear included."

"Okay. Yes, sir," Tyler replied, sounding tired and as if he didn't want to go back in the hospital room and tell Dori's parents that he needed to take yet another thing from her.

"Well, okay, then. Keep me posted," said Curtis. Then he hung up the phone, grabbed his coffee and a notepad, and headed for the interview room.

As he entered the room, he was confronted by one very upset architect who had traded his normal gentlemanly demeanor for that of a tyrant.

The six-by-six interview room contained a small gray metal table and three metal chairs. One with manners would call these furnishings retro, but the truth is that they were just old, worn, and uncomfortable. Someone years ago had placed a cushion on one of the chairs, but it had long since worn out in the middle. One of the sides was torn and had begun to fray. The light gray paint only added to the beauty of the space, giving the room the warm feeling of a prison.

Detective Curtis calmly walked into the room and quietly sat on the cushioned chair at the far end of the interview table.

Lawson, who had been pacing, stopped in his tracks as the detective entered. He watched him silently take a seat at the small metal table. Lawson stared at the detective, detesting his very existence. From the detective's worn-out dress shoes and similar shade of brown slacks, all the way to his white-collared polo-type shirt and disheveled hair, it was clear to Lawson that this cop didn't put much stock in his appearance.

Lawson was right, too. Curtis didn't spend an awful lot of time worrying about how he appeared. At the end of a day like this one, he could care less if he looked like one of his perps. After all, he had become an officer shortly after high school. Of course, it was just for the campus police at LSU, where he worked full time while working toward his criminal justice degree. Then he moved to New Orleans to join the big leagues—the New Orleans Police Department. He had made detective within six years. He was a good cop. No, he was a great cop. He didn't let his poor fashion choices prevent him from doing great detective work.

He was tall, a little over six feet, and, while he was slender, he certainly wasn't thin. He was muscular mostly because of his genetics, although he made a point to hit the gym several times a week. There, he spent as much time socializing with the other officers as he did working out. With brown hair and blue eyes, he was handsome—not pretty, but certainly handsome.

While the captain urged his detectives to wear suits, Curtis preferred dress slacks and polo shirts, especially at night when the captain dropped in only occasionally. During the day, he wore the full suit without complaint and looked like any other briefcase-toting lawman at the office (minus the jacket, which he usually left hanging on a hanger in the backseat of his car). Although he would describe himself as average, he was hardly average. Compared to Lawson, you might think that Curtis lacked a certain sophistication. But what he lacked there, he made up for with a sense of humor, an amazing loyalty, and a subtle humility that made him most everyone's best friend.

The detective took another sip of his coffee before placing the cup on the table. The ceramic, when it hit the metal, made a clanging sound which echoed in the room's silence. Curtis then placed his notepad on the table and casually dropped his pen on top of it. He sat back in his chair, crossed an ankle over one knee, leaned back, and folded his arms, looking directly at Lawson.

Incredulous when confronted with the detective's calm demeanor, Lawson stopped pacing, glared at Curtis, and then demanded, "What the fuck am I doing here? Is this some kind of fucked-up joke? You said I was going to the hospital. I've got rights, you know!" He paced the floor, red-faced and yelling, outburst-like: "Who does Curtis think he is, anyway? Curtis is a liar with a badge," he said. Curtis sat calmly, sipping his coffee.

When Lawson took a break, Curtis looked at his watch and said, "Okay, you've managed to waste another six minutes of both of our lives." Lawson paused, looking confused and contemplating the detective's words. Then he stood still, sighing heavily.

Next, leaning forward intently and looking directly into Lawson's eyes, Curtis said, "I found an injured, bleeding, and crying child in your arms. At your house. Did you really think I wasn't going to ask you how she got there?"

He let the last of his words hang in the air as he leaned back, crossed his arms again, and maintained his gaze into Lawson's eyes, as if waiting for a response.

Lawson looked closely at the detective, who could see evidence of reason creeping across Lawson's face. Lawson didn't respond; he just sort of stood there, looking at Curtis. After a few moments, Curtis raised his hand and indicated that Lawson join him at the table.

As Lawson reluctantly accepted the invitation, he said, "How's the baby?"

"Truthfully, I can't really say," responded Curtis with a shrug. "She's at the hospital, and her parents made it. She may be there a while."

When the word *parents* drifted from Curtis's mouth, Lawson turned his head quickly to look at the detective, his eyebrows raised in a question.

"Can I call Harold?" Lawson asked quietly. Without waiting for a response, he put both elbows on the table and buried his face in his hands. He seemed to stop breathing until the sound of a deep sob snuck from behind his hands.

Curtis, a bit humbled by Lawson's reaction, paused before speaking. "No. Not until we talk," he responded truthfully.

"What's the use?" came from behind the hands, which then began to move and wipe his eyes. "What the hell can I say to him, anyway?" It struck Curtis at that moment that this was not the type of man who cries often. In fact, he'd probably deny crying at all, choosing instead to say things like, "Something's in my eye."

"Well," started Curtis, "if you answer me honestly, this can be a short interview." He paused before saying, in a lighter tone, "If not, I'm going to need more coffee and you're going to need a pillow, because we're going to be here all night."

"Question me?" asked Lawson, confusion in his tone and eyes. "Question me?" he said again. This time his tone reflected the beginning of his realization. "Wait a minute. What the hell is this? You don't think ... no way, just ... me ... I ... no way." Lawson shook his head in disbelief.

"Listen, I don't know what happened at your house. Do I think you committed the crime? Maybe. Maybe not," Curtis said, shrugging. "Let's just start the best way I know how, all right?"

"Yeah, great," said Lawson sarcastically. "What do you want to know?"

"Well," said Curtis, squirming and getting comfortable in his seat, "start at the beginning."

"Which one?"

Curtis sighed, cocking his head to the side and addressing Lawson in a tone one would use if speaking to an invalid. "How do you know the Dauzats?" he questioned.

Lawson paused and looked into space as if the answer was encoded in the ceiling and he was trying to locate the answer key.

"Well, I've known Harold since I can remember," Lawson began. "Literally. We went to grade school together, Brother Martin High School, and eventually LSU. Actually, we pledged the same fraternity at LSU. Ended up being roommates." Lawson hesitated, then became quieter. "We've been the best of friends since. Lived together until he married, in fact. Actually, lived together after he was married, for nearly a year."

Lawson paused for a second, recollecting. "Especially since we started college, we've, uh, been the best of ... friends." His eyes shifted, his face reddening. He cleared his throat. It was obvious to Curtis that he was fighting back tears.

Curtis gave him a second to pull himself together. "What fraternity?" Curtis asked—not that he really cared which fraternity, but because he thought that a change in subject might lighten the heavy atmosphere of the room. Something about Lawson pulled at Curtis's gut. Although it was an occupational hazard, he felt some compassion for him. Lawson just looked so pathetic sitting there.

Lawson drew his breath in and said with a sigh, "Teke. We were Tekes."

Curtis's expression was blank.

"Tau Kappa Epsilon," Lawson offered in explanation. "They call us Tekes for short." Still receiving no real response from Curtis, he shrugged his shoulders before continuing. "Anyway, I knew Laurie since high school, too. Well, not really in high school—Brother Martin is an all-boys' school, you know. But we'd have dances and things like that. Opportunities, I mean, to meet girls. Anyhow, Laurie and I had several mutual friends, and I remember seeing her a few times. It wasn't until college that I really got to know her, when she started dating Harold."

Lawson paused, searching the archives of his memory. "She was always sweet, you know. Laurie, I mean. Putting up with all of us guys took a special person. Pretty. Smart. It's not easy to find that kind of girl who'll take on her man's best friend and a whole gang of guys hanging out all the time. Me bringing dates in and out of her house. You know, we all moved in together after college. They announced their engagement right before that. We would joke that I was her engagement present."

He paused here, shaking his head. Then Lee asked, "Is that what you meant by the beginning?"

Curtis leaned one elbow on the edge of the table. "I suppose," he replied. "Now tell me about tonight."

Lawson shrugged his shoulders. "Laurie asked me a couple weeks ago if I could watch Dori while they went to the Mardi Gras ball. I didn't mind …"

"Have you ever babysat her before?" Curtis interrupted.

"Well, yes. I mean, many times. She's my godchild. I eat dinner at their house more than at my own. I go with them on family vacations. You know what I mean. Harold sees his real brother less than he sees me. Same with my brother. We're just really tight. Not *Brokeback Mountain* tight, but you know what I mean."

"I get it," said Curtis, "you're great friends. What about the kid?"

Lawson looked down at his hands. "Well, I don't know really what to say. I don't have kids, and I don't know how to say it, but …" Lawson stopped. He looked away.

After a long pause, he continued. "See, I was there the day she was born. I waited with Harold and Laurie in the birthing room. Until Laurie kicked me out because she couldn't stand me and Harold making jokes and talking sports while she went through those spurts of pain. I remember, though, after she was born, when they wheeled little Dori down the hall. As they got closer to us, I saw Harold. He had a strange look on his face, like he was scared to death. I mouthed to him that it was okay. And then, there she was. Dori. I think she was the prettiest baby I'd ever seen."

Lawson's voice began to crack, but he continued. "She was so small—and wrapped up so tight. We all watched through the window while they weighed her and measured her. I waited forever to see her cry. I just couldn't believe she was ours. You know, I mean, Harold's. It wasn't until the next day that I was able to hold her, though. In fact, Laurie framed one of the photographs for me and one for Dori's nursery. She still has the picture of us in her room." A large tear fell from each eye, which he quickly wiped away with the back of his hand. He leaned back in his chair and took a deep breath.

If he's lying, he's good, Curtis thought.

"Like I said," continued Lawson, "she's the closest thing I'll probably ever have to a kid. I really, I just love her, you know."

Curtis, who also had never had children, responded with, "Yeah, I know." Then he paused to let the moment pass before continuing. "So, you agreed to babysit, and then what?"

"Well, I picked her up at home because Laurie was running late," started Lawson.

"What time?" interrupted Curtis.

"Oh, I guess about three or so," Lawson responded. "Anyway, like I said, I picked her up. She had her …" he paused. One could almost see the lump in his throat, which he cleared before continuing. "She had her little Cinderella book bag that I had given her for Christmas. It has her name … it has her name across the top. Anyhow, I had to stop by the office, and then we grabbed some pizza. We went home, she put on her pajamas," he paused again, tears welling in his eyes, "jammies—that's what she calls them." Lawson was looking more and more upset, and his words were coming out slowly.

It struck Curtis that Lawson wasn't searching for words as if to avoid being caught in a lie, but rather that it was difficult for him to actually say the words, as if each one caused his mouth some kind of physical pain.

"She wanted to see 'Daddy's school days,' meaning some old photo albums I have in which there are several pictures of Harold and me growing up. She loves looking at those pictures." Lawson hung his head down. "I'd spend hours telling her the stories behind each picture. She never gets tired of hearing ..." Lawson's voice finally broke. He simply couldn't say another word.

His tears fell freely. The man who before never cried looked now unable to stop. He was heartsick. His arms hung at his side; his back was slouched. He looked like a rag doll a child had thrown onto a chair and left.

Curtis cleared his throat. "What time did she get to bed?"

"I guess it was near nine-thirty," he responded, nodding his head. "Past bedtime. Laurie scolded me when we left. 'Lee, this time she has to go to bed by nine—seriously, you always throw her off schedule.'" Lawson said, suddenly angry, "She should have yelled at me not to let her daughter die!"

With this, Lawson stood up and slammed his fists into the wall. He turned to kick the chair, his leg missing the seat but catching the edge of the leg. The tangle caused him to fall to the floor. He went down heavy. Curtis leapt from his chair.

He wasn't sure what he was going to do, so he ended up reacting to the fall by staring down at the broken man. He was surprised to see Lawson lying on the floor like that. He wasn't moving. Just lying there, broken. Sobbing uncontrollably.

Curtis sighed. He stood there, looking down at the heap of sobbing madness on the floor. He ran his fingers through his hair. "Hey, man. Look, she's not going to die, she's ... she's going to be ... fine. She's going to be fine."

Curtis looked at his watch. He had been in here for nearly an hour and had not yet heard anything he could use.

"Mr. Lawson, please. Have a seat. We need to finish this."

Lawson slowly rose to his feet, picked up his chair, and sat facing Curtis. His face was red, puffy, and wet. Mostly, though, he just looked tired. "What else?"

"So, she went to bed around nine-thirty. Did you bring her to bed, did she put herself to bed ..."

"No, no," Lawson interrupted. "We have a ritual on the nights she stays at my house. I sing a silly song while she brushes her teeth, then we read whatever book she brought, and then I tuck her in and hit play on the DVD. She usually falls asleep right away. I, on the other hand, usually wake up several times to check on her. In fact, I sleep with the light on, usually, so that I don't get too comfortable. I know that's weird. I'm not really paranoid. I guess there's just something nice about checking on her. Pulling the covers up around her, that sort of thing."

"Is that what you did tonight?" the detective asked.

"Yeah, pretty much."

Curtis paused. "Was her window open?"

"No."

"Did anyone come over?"

Lawson shook his head. "No."

"Then what'd you do—after she went to bed, I mean?"

"I went to bed."

Thinking out loud, Curtis said, "So, when did you notice that something was wrong?"

"Well, I checked on her after I changed clothes for bed and, you know, brushed my teeth and went to the bathroom, that kind of thing. She was already asleep. Her doll had fallen off the bed, and I put it back next to her. Then I went to bed, read a book for a while, and dozed off.

"It must have been around eleven or so when something woke me up. At the time, I thought it was just noise on the street. Like I said, I usually sleep pretty light when the baby sleeps over. I flipped the channels a couple of times, and then thought I'd check on Dori.

"I knew right away, when I came around the corner and didn't see her feet but saw that the blankets were pulled down. I can't explain it. Panic right away. I guess it was a gut feeling. Anyway, as I walked into the room, I started saying, 'Dori? Dori? Where are you, Dori?' and there was nothing. Silence. The room felt ice-cold. I checked the bathroom, but I don't think I even went all the way in. The lights were off. I just knew she wasn't there.

"I ran down the stairs, yelling her name. The lights were still off, so I just kept going, right through the living room and into the kitchen, and then I finally saw the motion-sensor light on in the backyard. When I saw that light, I was thinking, *Please, please, please,* you know. Like, *Please let her be there.* And there she was."

At this point, Lawson's voice began to break once more. He looked down at the table, his whole face telling the story of his grief. "There she was," he repeated.

"Where exactly was she?" Curtis asked quietly.

"At the bottom of the stairs," he said slowly, staring at the wall like it was a screen showing a terrible movie.

"At first," he continued, unprompted, "at first, I was relieved." Lawson's tears begin to fall. He wasn't sobbing or wailing. The tears just fell, quietly and unnoticed by Lawson. He spoke slowly and dramatically. "I was relieved. It lasted only a fraction of a second. Just a fraction.

"I opened the screen door slowly. I could see her lying there, her head near the base of the stairs. Her body was lying flat, with her hands taped and clenched together and with just her little fingers showing. Her legs straight out, with just her feet sticking out of the bottom of her nightgown.

"I came out onto the porch. She didn't move. She was so stiff-looking. I thought she was dead. I couldn't see her face. Her hair covered most of it. Just small parts of her chin peeking from behind what looked like a blonde veil.

"As I came down the steps, I saw the blood. Strange, but I remember that she had blood on the tip of one of her fingers. I began to bend down near her face. I was scared to touch her.

"'Dori,' I said. 'Dori, dear God, Dori.' She didn't respond. Nothing. I knew she was dead. I moved her hair from her face. She didn't move.

"Her face felt warm. I put my cheek to her mouth and, finally, after what seemed like years, I could feel her soft breath touch my cheek.

"'Dori,' I yelled as I put my arms under her broken body and picked her up. Her eyes moved, and I saw a flash of recognition in her eyes. She started to cry. Just a small, soft, deep cry.

"I guess I panicked. I brought her inside and called 9-1-1. I just held her on the couch until they got there. I couldn't bring myself to put her down."

There was a long pause.

Finally, Curtis asked, "Did she say anything?"

"Not a word. Not a single word," Lawson responded, rubbing his eyes with the back of his hand.

Curtis sat watching Lawson for a long time. He was measuring his words, trying to get a solid read on him. Finally, he said, "Who did it?"

Lawson turned his head quickly to the detective and, without hesitation, said, "I don't know." Looking down at his hands and shaking his head, he said, "I don't know what sick bastard did this. He better hope you find him before I do."

Curtis shrugged his shoulders while saying, "Well, do you have any enemies?"

"I've been in business for years now; I suppose I've earned a few enemies. They'd smile at me while stealing an account from under me, without any hesitation. But hurt a kid to get even with me? No. No, I don't have any enemies like that."

"What about Harold?" asked Curtis, sighing.

"No, no. Couldn't be."

"What about this girl of yours, the one you raped in high school?"

Lawson's eyebrows arched in surprise—shock, even. Then they quickly indented in anger. "Are you fucking kidding me? Is this some kind of sick joke?" Lawson scoffed.

"Sure, yeah," Curtis said, taking a swig of coffee. "I'm sure your victim thinks it's hilarious." Curtis knew he was provoking Lawson, but so far, nothing. It was time to be bad cop to his own good cop.

Lawson leaned forward, resting his elbows on his knees. He put his hands together and looked Curtis in his eyes. His tone was one of restrained anger when he said, "My *victim*? *She's* the victim?"

Lawson leaned back in his chair and shook his head slowly. "I haven't talked about this in years. I'm going to tell you this story once. Then I'm leaving to see Dori, unless you arrest me. And if I read about this shit in the paper tomorrow, I'll know whom to file my slander suit against.

"I was sixteen years old, a sophomore in high school. I was dating this girl and got to know her better in the backseat of my dad's car. Actually, that wasn't the only place. We were very active, if you know what I mean. About a month later, she tells me she thinks she's pregnant. We scrounge fifteen bucks together to buy a drugstore test. It was positive.

"Monday, I get called into the school office. The police are there, the principal, my parents—and then I saw her. Sitting there, looking pathetic, with her parents next to her. Principal says that she told them I raped her and got her pregnant.

"She couldn't even look at me. Just sat there, all pitiful and stuff. Police said they were investigating the matter. Principal suspended me, pending the outcome of the investigation.

"About a week later, I find a white envelope on my windshield. It's a letter from her. Says that she was scared to tell her parents that she was having sex and had become pregnant. She knew she'd get in trouble unless she said she was raped. The letter begged me not to tell anyone because she thought her parents would send her to live with her grandparents out of state.

"Shit, I took that letter right to my parents, and together we went to the police. She got suspended. Never came back. either. I guess her

25

parents sent her to her grandmother's. I didn't care. I was so pissed. Thought she was trying to ruin my life."

"What happened to the baby?" Curtis asked.

"My mom told me that her parents called and said that she miscarried less than a month later."

"Hm," Curtis responded, thinking to himself.

"You know, for years I had people ask me about that girl. I know in the back of their minds they still wondered if I did it." He leaned back in his chair. "I hated her for years for that." Lawson shook his head slowly and crossed his arms. "It was just several years ago that I came to terms with what happened. I know now that she was just a scared kid, you know?"

"I guess so."

Both men were silent for a few moments.

"Well, anything to add?" Curtis finally asked.

Lawson shrugged. "Not that I can think of. Except maybe the tape. I pulled the tape off her hands. It was near the couch."

"We got it. Anything else?"

Lawson just shook his head and glanced at his watch.

"Well, I guess you should know that Dori's at the hospital. She isn't talking yet." Then, pointing at Lawson, he added, "But when she does, I'll be there. Your story better check out."

Lawson replied, in a tone of pure disgust, "Give me a fucking break."

CHAPTER 3

IT WASN'T LONG AFTER LAWSON HAD LEFT THAT HE HAD WALKED—no, stalked—right back into the child abuse unit. Putting a hand on his hip and huffing, he said, "Can I get a ride, or what?"

Curtis, who was sitting quietly at his desk, raised his head to see the aggravated architect staring back. He arched his eyebrows in a questioning manner.

"Give me a break, okay. You brought me here with no car, and it's not like you can get a cab in this shitty neighborhood," said Lawson, the volume of his voice rising.

The detective couldn't help but give a faint smile and nod. "Sure. I mean, no problem." Curtis grabbed his keys and notepad and started walking toward to door. "Actually, I was going to stop at the hospital on my way home, anyway." Curtis passed Lawson and headed out the doorway.

"Great," responded Lawson dryly.

The ride to the hospital seemed unending to both of them. It was as if they were constantly behind the slowest car and catching every red light.

They didn't speak. Curtis held onto the steering wheel tightly with both hands and stared intently through the windshield.

If asked to recall what he saw along the drive, he would have very little to offer. It consisted of staring at the blacktop ahead and relentlessly passing the white dashed lines on the road. The occasional flashing of a streetlight. It was just another day among his many long days as a detective.

Lawson, on the other hand, watched out the passenger window. His eyes took in the deadness of the city. He watched the shadows change on the office buildings as the car passed. He caught the eye of a streetwalker or two along the way, his sharp eyes seeing, but not really.

Neither man intentionally ignored the other. They were both simply consumed in thought.

Curtis's thoughts were wrapped around the case. He was uneasy with Lawson as his primary suspect. The puzzle wasn't fitting together yet. Lawson had no real priors. Curtis knew from experience that most people don't just go from zero to rape in one night, especially when they know that under the circumstances they are the first likely suspect.

If a stranger had been casing the residence, then how did they know the little girl would be there? This was obviously a purely sex-related crime. There was nothing stolen, no one else hurt. Could it be someone who intended to kidnap the girl for purposes of extortion? But who, and why did they leave her there to die instead of removing her from the scene?

Lawson's thoughts, on the other hand, were wrapped around his friends, his family. He couldn't wait to get to the hospital. Yet, at the same time, he dreaded his arrival at the hospital. What was he going to say? What was Harold going to say? Could Laurie forgive him? Could he forgive himself? Damn. Damn it.

Finally, there it was. Magnolia Hospital. The green sign glowed against the black backdrop of night. Curtis pulled his car into the police zone near the emergency room's entrance. Neither man reached for a door handle.

Finally, Curtis said, "So, here we are," matter-of-factly. Without another word, or even a response, both started to get out of the car.

Neither looked at the other. Had they, Lawson would have seen a look of confusion on the detective's face, and Curtis would have seen a look of pain and anticipation on Lawson's face.

As they approached the emergency room, the sliding glass door glided open to reveal a large receiving area. The room was brightly lit. Several people bustled about, and several others sat in torn waiting-room chairs.

Curtis headed straight to the nurses' desk while Lawson stopped just inside the doorway. *So, this is Magnolia,* he thought. He feverishly searched each face. *Where is she, and where are they?*

"Lawson!" Detective Curtis yelled out to him, trying to get his attention. "This way," he motioned.

Lawson joined him at the desk. "She's in room three-oh-nine. Now, look, and I'm not screwing around here, I'm going to let you go in with me, but no messing around. If the kid or the parents want you out or start freaking out or something, you're out of there."

Curtis looked at Lawson's face for some sort of indication. Seeing only a face full of anticipation, he demanded, "You got me, Lawson?"

"Yeah, I got you. Let's get on with this."

The two of them began their journey down a long corridor. Curtis pointed at his badge to indicate to the guard standing at the entrance that he was a police officer. If Lawson noticed the guard or Curtis, he didn't let it show. Instead, he looked nervously from door to door, reading each number, as if Dori's room might just appear out of order.

They walked slowly but determinedly: 301, 303, 305, 307, and then 309.

Room 309. The white door was open just a crack. Lawson noticed that the inside of the room was darker than the corridor. One could see the flicker of blue light bouncing off the wall. Lawson knew in an instant that the television was on, despite the fact that there was no sound.

Curtis and Lawson stood staring at the door. Finally, Lawson turned and looked at Curtis. They were arguing silently about who was going to open that door and expose the fact to this family that yet another cop, along with the man who was accused of hurting their daughter, was there to visit.

Curtis won.

Lawson slowly pushed the door open and took one step inside. Dori lay covered in white sheets up to her underarms. Compared to Dori's small frame, the hospital bed seemed large and overwhelming. The child appeared to be sleeping quietly. Lawson's eyes, moving farther down the bed, spotted Dori's mother, Laurie, on the opposite side, sitting in a chair. He could see that her hand was outstretched, holding Dori's hand, which lay on the baby's belly. Laurie's head was facedown on the blanket, at Dori's side. Neither moved when Lawson opened the door.

After gazing at them for a moment, his eyes continued their search for the missing person. His gaze finally found its mark in the eyes of Harold, who had apparently been standing near the door and watching Lawson the whole time.

Harold's eyes asked the question, *Did you ... could you have?*

Lawson's eyes asked the question, *Can you forgive me?*

"I ... I ... Harold, I don't know what to say," said Lawson, breaking the silence.

Harold didn't respond, just shook his head side to side, tears beginning to fall down his cheeks. His eyes never left Lawson's.

Finally, Harold crossed the room quickly. Curtis pushed to get past Lawson, trying to get in front of him, intending to protect him from Harold's attack.

Before Curtis could intervene, though, Harold grabbed Lawson and put his arms around him. Both men cried. Lawson said, "Is she going to live?"

"Yes, yes," Harold responded.

Lawson began falling to his knees, holding onto Harold's arm. Squatting right there in the entrance, he sobbed uncontrollably. Lawson covered his face and could hardly breathe. Harold squatted next to him and put his hand on his friend's back.

"What the hell am I going to do?" said Harold. "What the hell am I going to do? What the hell am I going to do?"

Lawson shook his head and wiped his eyes with the back of his hand. Glancing up at Dori, he came to realize that Laurie was now standing on the side of Dori's bed nearest the door. Her arms were crossed. Tears streamed down her face. She was staring at Lawson, her eyes questioning him.

"Laurie," Lawson whispered. He opened his mouth to say something to her, something comforting, but nothing came out. As his mind searched for words, he was distracted by the movement right behind her.

His breath caught in his lungs. He was unable to speak and, instead, stood straight up, mouth open in shock, and pointed at the bed.

Laurie and Harold turned to look at their daughter.

The child lay still on the hospital bed. Her blonde hair covered the pillow like a halo around her head. Her face was turned toward the door. She was watching them! Her eyes pleaded with Lawson as a tear began to make its slow journey down her face. Her body lay motionless, save for her tiny chest, which moved in a slow but steady rhythm.

Slowly, she began to lift her hand. Then her arm followed. She extended her hand as if she were going to point at something. Her index finger seemed to be extended, the palm of her small hand pointing downward.

Curtis thought, *If she points at him, I'm arresting his ass.*

Her hand slowly passed her mother, passed her father, and stopped at Lawson. Then, she slowly began to turn her hand so that her palm pointed upward. The small, quiet child turned her hand completely around, as if she were extending her hand to him! Her small eyebrows were arched, and her eyes looked apologetically at Lawson.

Laurie turned quickly to Lawson and, before another minute passed, put her arms around him, hugging him tightly. "I'm sorry, I

just wasn't sure. I just didn't know. I didn't think it was you, I just …
I…," she stammered. She looked back at her daughter, whose little
hand was still extended. "Go to her, Lee."

Lawson, whose eyes had never left the small child, walked to
the bed and grabbed the child's hand. "My sweet princess. My baby.
I won't leave your side. I let you down, I know I let you down." He
began sobbing again. "I'll fix this for you, baby. I will. I'm sorry …
forgive me, forgive me." He laid his head on her belly, begging for
forgiveness and sobbing uncontrollably.

The child took his hand, still stained with the blood of her
innocence, and pulled it to her chest. Lawson climbed onto the edge
of the bed while holding her hand. He spoke to her quietly. "I let you
down, honey. I let you down. I found you too late." The tears welled
in his eyes; he choked on every word. "You're safe now. I promise,
you're safe now."

Looking in her eyes, and with all the sincerity of the world
in his voice, he continued. "I promise you, though, I will spend
the rest of my life making it right for you. I won't fail you again.
I'll make it right. I'll make it right," he stammered over and over
again, crying.

Dori only listened to a few sentences before falling asleep.
Another tear rolled down her soft, pink cheek. Lee gently wiped the
tear and then lay his head next to hers on the pillow as he curled up
beside her, saying, "I'll catch every tear, honey. I won't let another
fall, not on my watch. Every tear." His eyes were closed and there
was a pained look on his face.

Laurie quietly resumed her spot on the other side of the bed,
holding Dori's other hand, while Harold quietly resumed his spot
near the door, determined that no one would get in. No one would
hurt his family again—not without getting past him.

It was at this point that he noticed the detective.

Curtis, who had quietly watched the events unfold, remained in
the doorway without making his presence known. Curtis, who had

not yet said a word, nodded at Harold and slowly closed the door behind himself.

There was nothing to say. The truth was obvious. It was clear to Curtis that the reason the baby lay in a hospital bed had nothing to do with the man who was lying next to her. The batterer was still out there ... somewhere.

CHAPTER 4

"DETECTIVE CURTIS, NOPD," CURTIS ANSWERED HIS DESK PHONE. It had been a couple of days since he first received the call about Dori Dauzat—and just as long since he last slept.

"Hey, Brad. It just came in. Perfect match to a … eh … Bruce Gurganus, spelled G-U-R," said the voice on the other end of the line.

Curtis interrupted. "I have the spelling. It's the same name that came back once the prints were run. This is great, Connor, I appreciate the rush. The match locks it up for me. This guy is a sick bastard, you know?"

Connor Lewis was the chief forensic medical examiner for the coroner's office. "Yeah, I heard the facts. Sick puppy. Who's the ADA?" Connor asked.

"Sandra Morgan's been assigned, thank goodness."

"For more reason than one, I'm sure," Connor replied with a chuckle. "She makes it hard for me to testify, what with prancing her pretty little butt all around the courtroom!"

"Speaking of sick puppies," Curtis began.

"Hey, I'm happily married. You, on the other hand, need a woman or a hobby. I'd try for the woman first, if I were you," Connor said, humor filling his voice.

"Nice," Curtis replied sarcastically. "Advice from the man who spends his day with dead people! Catch ya later."

After hanging up, Curtis spent several hours preparing his report. Later that day, he called Sandra to discuss the case with her—over coffee.

CHAPTER 5

"STATE VERSUS GURGANUS," SANDRA MORGAN REPLIED ONCE THE judge had inquired where they were on the docket. Her finger had glided past many names before coming to rest on this particular one. The docket, a written list containing the names and case numbers of every matter pending before the court on any single day, was arranged numerically, in the order in which a case happened to be assigned to this division of the criminal court system. The docket, scribbled with Morgan's notes, was eight pages long and named seventy-nine defendants. Her finger had come to rest on docket number seventy-six.

As her finger and attention hovered over docket number seventy-six, she sighed with relief. *Nearly done,* she thought to herself.

Working in the district attorney's office in New Orleans had never been an easy task. Sandra Morgan, an assistant district attorney (ADA) for Orleans Parish, had been assigned to division H for several months. Her assignment had followed her promotion to the felony section of the district attorney's office. The promotion was well-deserved, given her intense dedication and successful trial record.

The district attorney's office wasn't exactly beauty school. The huge caseload and low pay had run off many good lawyers. But Sandy knew that this job was her calling—a calling she felt compelled to answer. She had worked tirelessly in her four years as an ADA handling simple burglaries, crimes against nature, petty theft, and other low-key crimes. Eventually, she was assigned to simple felonies, for example, batteries, assaults, crimes against peace officers, and too many drug violations to count.

Her reputation as a trial attorney was recognized and appreciated. Outside of trial, she was willing to work out a quick plea, which went a long way with the defense attorneys. Most of them, like Sandy, needed these cases to move along—and both sides usually knew the score after a quick review of the evidence. Sandy was normally able to give the evidence a cursory look and know right then and there if she had enough for a conviction or not. There was no need to play games; just get down to business.

At the same time, Sandy didn't mind going to trial. With a number of trials under her belt, she had found that they weren't quite as difficult as some of the veterans pretended they were. Sandy's superiors claimed that she didn't mind going to trial simply because of her rising conviction rate, like she was trying to break an unknown record. And while it was true that she did enjoy a trial record envied by many, it was not the number of convictions that had made her memorable.

Simply put, Sandy stood out. When she walked into a room, people's eyes simply seemed drawn to her. There was something different about her. Something special. Not quite spectacular, but just … interesting. One could feel her energy.

This is not to say that she stood out for a particular reason. She was neither loud nor demanding. Her petite, five-and-a-half-foot frame was hardly intimidating. Yet beneath her gentle sarcasm and quick wit was something understated and unique.

The truth was that she was strikingly beautiful. She didn't possess the type of beauty one would find in a magazine model. No, her beauty was subtle. She had dark hair, deep brown eyes, and soft features. She appeared younger than her twenty-nine years. Class was written all over her.

Sandy was always impeccably dressed. She wasn't flashy, and her clothes weren't especially expensive, but she was always put together well, as if she had planned every detail of the simple suits she wore. Although her appearance was generally conservative, her expensive, sassy shoes told a different story.

While one's eyes might have been drawn by her appearance, it wouldn't take long for a person to realize that Sandy's beauty was equally matched by her brains.

Her male counterparts at the office often teased her about her appearance. "It's a trap," they would say, laughing. "She appears sweet and nice, and then she opens her mouth and pure hell pours out." Sandy was single and hadn't had a serious boyfriend since college. She took their jabs lightheartedly, shrugging and laughing them off.

It was no secret to Sandy that her appearance helped her in the courtroom. It was clear to her that, in many ways, it gave her instant credibility. She looked easy to approach yet professional—just as she had intended. She was pretty enough to get people's attention, but not so pretty that they were afraid to talk to her.

However, she also knew that the reason for her success was something that went much deeper than her looks. Since she had been a child, there was always something about her that made people want to be near her, to help her, and to be part of her life.

Juries were no different. She would approach the jury to make her opening statement and begin speaking in her soft, nurturing voice. She would encourage them to use common sense and remind them that this was their case and their decision. Almost always, she would state that she was "just a tool to aid them in finding the truth."

The juries immediately responded to her, watched her, and trusted her. One could see them physically respond to her; they leaned forward in their seats, gave subtle nods, and even winked on occasion.

When the defense attorney, usually a man, had the opportunity to try to disenchant the jury members, he almost always realized that it was too late. She would have had them from the word *go*.

But there was no jury there today, just Sandy, the judge, his staff, a couple of defense attorneys, a public defender, and the four remaining defendants. This was an arraignment day. The defendants were read the formal charges alleged against them by the State. They would then enter their pleas of guilty, not guilty, or not guilty by reason of insanity. Then the court would assign the date when it would hear any motions as well as a trial date. Within minutes, the process was complete, at which point the court was ready to move on to docket number seventy-seven.

Sandy rarely read the cases before the day of arraignment. Prior to the arraignment, the cases were screened by an entry-level ADA and then funneled through the system until they landed in her file cabinet, awaiting the next step. At the arraignment, Sandy would open each file for the first time, jot down the plea and the defense attorney's name, and then tuck the file back in the stack with the others to prepare plea agreements or motions—or for trial.

Sandy glanced at the judge as she reached for number seventy-six's file. She could see the frustration on his face as he searched his copy of the docket.

"Where did you say we were, Counselor?" he asked in his deep voice, which had an even deeper Southern accent. His eyebrows arched as he flipped the pages of the docket.

Judge Curtis Bryson had been on the bench for close to fourteen years. He was a large, heavyset man in his late sixties. He was quick with a smile and tended to take a no-nonsense, common-sense approach to these cases, although he always seemed to be a bit confused or somewhat distracted. Just when Sandy thought he needed to adjust his medication, he said something brilliant and reminded everyone that he belonged there. Sandy knew that a procedural-type day such as this one required little of his attention, as everyone was just going through the motions of getting the arraignments done. Still, as usual, he had lost his place on the docket.

Judge Bryson sat high above his staff, who were seated just below him. The minute clerk would enter into her small notebook computer the action that had been taken that day in court, and the court reporter steadily recorded and transcribed the spoken event. The two gave each other knowing glances. The court reporter rolled her eyes as if to say, *Here we go again.*

"Number seventy-six, Your Honor. Would you like me to call the case and proceed?" Sandy responded, smiling softly at his blunder.

"Oh yes, I see," he said, relief smoothing his brow as he located the proper case. "Please proceed, Ms. Morgan."

Sandy pulled the brand new brown file from the small stack of files for the remaining cases. The tab had a new label bearing the case title, but across the front of the file, the clerk's office had written the full title in a black felt marker. It was from here that she read, *State of Louisiana v. Bruce Gurganus.*

She opened the file to the bill of information and continued to read. "The State of Louisiana has charged the defendant, namely Bruce Gurganus, as follows: count one, sexual assault of a minor, namely Adorina Dauzat, age five; count two, carnal knowledge of a juvenile, namely Adorina Dauzat, age five; and count three, forcible rape of a juvenile, namely Adorina Dauzat, age five."

With this last count, Sandy began to scribble today's date onto the note section of the open file. Then she paused to hear the defendant's plea so that she could enter it into her notes.

"Counsel, make your appearance for the record," said the judge.

Sandy raised her head to watch the defense attorney approach. Truthfully, she rarely noticed anyone else in the courtroom, particularly during arraignments when the goal was to get through a huge docket before lunchtime. It reminded her of a cattle call, with the judge's bellowing, "Next," so that he could finish up and make it to the golf course, at which point she could go back to her office to prepare for the inevitable barrage of trials the next day.

Now, however, nearly at the end of the day, she did take the opportunity to glance up just in time to behold the familiarly slow gait of a most bothersome opponent. "May it please the court," he said in his slow, gruff voice, "Robert Samuel, on behalf of the defendant, Bruce Gurganus, who is present and in the courtroom."

The judge and Samuel exchanged smiles and nods without attempting to disguise the fact that the two knew each other. New Orleans's was, however, a small legal community, so these types of exchanges were commonplace and generally went ignored.

"Mr. Samuel, did you hear the charges against your client as read by the State?" asked the judge.

"Why, most certainly, sir," Samuel replied.

This was one of Samuel's typical responses. Most attorneys addressed such a miniscule formality quickly and to the point, saying, "Yes, and we'd like to enter a plea of not guilty." Samuel, however, moved slowly and steadily, with absolutely no speed or urgency, as if he intended at least to appear that he was giving his client his money's worth. For someone like Sandy, who was quick and precise, Samuel's unnecessary delays tested her patience.

"Are you prepared to enter your plea?" asked the judge.

"We would, Your Honor, but first, may we approach the bench?" replied Samuel. The judge motioned for the defense attorney to approach. Sandy sighed as she glanced at her watch. Her mind was filled with the long list of things remaining for her to do before she could go home.

There were two tables at which the attorneys sat in the courtroom. Both faced the judge's bench. At Sandy's table sat Sandy, her law clerk, and three boxes containing the seventy-nine new files. To the left of her was the defense's table, where usually the public defender and various defense attorneys sat awaiting their turn. Farther left, next to the defense's table, were a couple rows of seats where the defendants awaited to learn their fate. As a defendant's case was called, he or she was moved to the defense's table until the matter to be addressed that day was resolved. Then, the defendant was taken straight to the holding cell just outside of the courtroom, again to wait—this time for their trip back to jail.

Behind the tables was a long rail running the width of the courtroom, separating the audience of defendants and witnesses from the front of the courtroom. In the middle of this rail was a swinging entry gate. To the right of Sandy's table was the jury box containing two rows of seven seats each, which was just enough seating for the twelve members of a jury and two alternates. The jury seats, which matched those at the counselors' and courtroom staff's tables, were made of the same shade of cherry wood as the rail, the tables, and the judge's bench. The inside of this courtroom reminded Sandy of an old study. She thoroughly enjoyed the room's atmosphere of formality and seriousness.

Truth be known, she actually loved this room because of its proper décor, its high ceilings that highlighted her strong voice as it bounced across the room, and the respect it commanded.

Sandy reluctantly stood up from her chair, walked to the foot of the judge's bench, and up the two stairs to reach the judge's podium. She leaned comfortably next to the judge, as she had done many times before. She began to flip through the file for the first time as Samuel began his dance. Samuel stood before the judge in his overpriced suit that had been carefully tailored to fit him perfectly. In an effort to show off the cuffs of his shirt, which bore his initials, he had developed a habit of constantly pulling at his cuff links as he spoke. His cuff links were gold with diamond accents. If one looked more closely, one would notice that his button covers were gold, too.

Sandy looked loathingly at Samuel. It wasn't that he was a bad-looking man. In fact, she thought, had his picture been in an upscale magazine, she would probably admire him. He was thin, tall, and too tan, and he had the type of silky, solid gray hair that usually came from a bottle. The problem was that this wasn't a magazine. This was a courtroom. The way he casually walked in and out, with his flashy attire and blasé attitude, bothered Sandy. She would much prefer that he regarded the setting as seriously as she did.

True to his reputation, Samuel began issuing a barrage of niceties at the judge. He thanked him profusely for coming to speak at an organization of which Samuel was the president, and he stressed what a wonderful job the judge had done. He said that he was impressed by the judge's knowledge. After this, he told the judge that he had been reminded of a time in law school when the two had taken a weekend trip to protest at a different university. And so on.

Sandy patiently read through the file. When she finished, she again glanced at her watch, saying, "Well, I hate to be a party pooper, but ..."

"Oh yes, pardon us for catching up," Samuel said. The words were directed at Sandy, but he didn't bother himself to actually look at her when he spoke them. To him, she was just another one in a long line of young assistant district attorneys—certainly not worthy of his precious courtesy.

"You see, Judge, I happen to know this defendant personally. That is to say, sir, that I know his mother really well." Samuel tugged at his cuffs before crossing his arms, as if he were about to make a very important statement. "His mother is a legal secretary in my office and has been with me for a number of years. I can vouch for this family. A very nice bunch and quite respected in the community. In fact, you may have heard of his father, Robert Gurganus."

"The architect?" interrupted the judge.

"Yes, sir—did that lovely job designing that new museum on Broad Street, you know, the ... well"—he continued, while crossing his arms across his chest and shaking his head—"the name of it escapes me now. Anyhow, Judge, they have a lovely family, just lovely. In fact, just last week I hosted ..."

Sandy interrupted. "With all due respect, and pardon the interruption, but, frankly, I don't care how nice the defendant is or to whom he is related. The bottom line is that a little five-year-old girl said he raped her. And someone believed her, because the police arrested him. The case was screened and the charges were accepted. So, here we sit. Unless this is a case of mistaken identity, I suggest we move on."

Samuel stared at her blankly while the judge nodded. "Yes, yes, let's move forward. It's just the arraignment, Bob." He turned his attention to Samuel. "Unless you have something else to add?"

Samuel shook his head side to side as he began to speak. "Well, I was just in hopes that we may reach some kind of understanding today. Perhaps with the court's encouragement, the State would be happy to discuss a reduction of the charges."

"I'd be happy to discuss a plea," Sandy replied before the judge had the opportunity, "just not here and not today. Call me or drop by, but I need to wrap this up today—big trial tomorrow."

"Actually," Samuel persisted, "I was thinking that perhaps the court would aid in a making a little adjustment today. You know, to show a little good faith on behalf of the State." He leaned his body toward the judge, smiled, and nodded.

Sandy made a move to begin telling him exactly where he could stuff that idea when she was cut off by the judge.

"Oh—no, sir," said the judge. "Not here and not from me. If you need to discuss something with me," he raised his eyebrows to highlight the fact that he was exaggerating, "unrelated to this case, of course [wink, wink], then perhaps we should meet later this week for lunch. But, just for the record, you try your case out there," he said, indicating with both hands that he meant the audience and the jury, "not here." He finished by resting his hands on his desk.

The judge shrugged his shoulders apologetically, as if to say that he would like to help but couldn't. "See, Bob," he said directly to Samuel, "there's been so much going on here that I have to be extremely careful." The judge, who looked over both shoulders as he spoke, was alluding to the recent public accusations against a fellow judge in a neighboring parish who had been videoed accepting a bribe. "Sometimes things are said that can be taken the wrong way. Let's just finish up what you have today."

"Yes, sir," both attorneys responded.

Sandy and Samuel walked back to their respective tables. Sandy sat in her seat and looked to her left to find Samuel leaning over to whisper something in his client's ear. She could see part of Samuel's face. He pulled at his cuffs again before moving his jacket back and placing one of his hands in his pocket. The other hand moved with his explanation.

The man he spoke to sat at the defendant's table. Sandra hadn't really noticed him before, but then she generally didn't pay particular attention to the defendants. After so many criminal trials, they all looked the same to her: faceless defendants in orange jumpers with the word *inmate* written in bold capital letters across the back.

She could see the man nodding affirmatively in response to what Samuel was whispering. His hair was more gray than black; it was in dire need of cutting. It just sat there on the back of his head, wiry and chaotic. His hands held each other tightly on the table in front of him. His ankles were crossed at the ends of his outstretched legs. He appeared to be comfortably slouching in the defense chair.

Sandy sighed again, aggravated by the waste of time and wondering what they could be discussing that would take this much time.

Finally, Samuel began to move his upper body away from the defendant. He turned completely around before beginning to speak. "Judge, we are prepared to enter our plea."

"Fine, uh … Mr., um …" the judge responded, his eyes searching, as he had again lost his place on the docket. "Oh yes, here, Mr. Gurganus," he continued, evidently having found the appropriate place. "Please rise."

The defendant began to rise. To support his weight, he placed his hands on the defense's table as his stood. As he did so, he turned his head to the right, looking Sandy in the eyes.

Sandy caught her breath. There was something so familiar about this man, and yet she couldn't quite place him. She knew him instantly—but from where? She looked away from his eyes; her glance fell to his hands.

The hands ... wait! Yet it couldn't be! Her chest tightened as she felt the air moving in and out of her lungs. It was heavy; she breathed with great effort. She actually felt her heart slow down as she came face-to-face with a memory so lost to her that she could scarcely believe it now.

She stared at Gurganus, her mouth open and her eyes wide with shock. She was utterly confused. Why is he so familiar? *No ... he couldn't be.* Her mind flooded with snapshots of her past.

She could see his dark hands. Short fingers with black, wiry hairs on the knuckles. His disheveled hair. His voice calling for her. "Want to play a game?" his deep sinister voice had taunted. She could see her mother's face, shocked and looking at her in disbelief, and her father with his head in his hands. The sound of his sobs. "But he was a friend," he repeated over and over, quietly. She could see her third grade classroom—the sympathy on her teacher's face before she put her arms around her. She could feel him—grabbing at her and then pulling at her. His hands were relentless. They pushed her down. She could smell the smoke on his clothes and on his breath as he repeated, "Don't talk. Don't talk, little one, don't talk."

How long had it been? How many years? She couldn't remember. Wouldn't remember. She was eight—only eight. In an instant, her past pulled her backward. She could see the microphone she had been asked to speak into. She remembered her mother and grandmother in the audience; they were weeping. Her mind recalled the judge's face as he read a white paper, and the lady in a suit next to her, feverishly shaking her head in disbelief. She remembered her mother grabbing her hand and pulling her out of the courtroom.

Sandy tore her eyes away from the defendant and looked back at the docket. Staring at his name, the thought occurred to her that she should scream. Should she scream? She looked to the back of the courtroom. The tall, wooden doors stood calling her. *Run. Run!* She looked back at him. He was staring at her. Her heart leapt to her throat. He was staring back at her. But his expression was blank.

Wait—his expression. It couldn't be. *He doesn't remember me?* her mind begged. She held her breath. *He doesn't remember me,* her heart resolved. *How many thousands of times had he come to me in a midnight dream—and he doesn't remember me!? Is this real? How dare he? How dare he!*

Her eyes jetted around the room to see if it was obvious to anyone else. Everyone was staring back at her. *It's obvious. They know,* she thought. She could feel her pulse panicking in each vein, as if the blood was crashing into her veins' walls as it darted for a place to hide.

"Ms. Morgan!" the judge exclaimed, aggravated. Her eyes, frantic, moved to regard him. "Are you with us?" His tone was one more of anger than of concern, as if the question were a reprimand.

"I'm …" she paused. She was confused. She should tell. She couldn't prosecute this case. The code of ethics demanded that she step down. But this was her chance, right? This was her chance to make him pay. Take the case or withdraw? "I'm fine," she said so slowly that it appeared she had to search long and hard for each word.

"Very well, what date would you like?" replied the judge, shaking his head.

"My apologies to the court," Sandy said, her voice still small, "but what was the plea?"

The judge removed his glasses as if to get a better look at her. He raised his eyebrows in disbelief as he began to speak slowly, as he might speak to a child. "Ms. Morgan, the defendant entered a plea of not guilty. We are in the process of picking a motions and trial date. Would you care to join us?"

"My apologies, Judge, I guess I was a little distracted. It's just…." Her voice trailed off. Sandy's eyes went to her calendar. This was her chance to speak up, her chance to be removed from this case, her chance to say out loud the things she hadn't been spoken of for more than a decade.

She could hear herself speaking, her body and voice on autopilot, while her mind was years and miles away. She said, "Today is the thirtieth, so how about June seventh for the motions hearing and August eleventh for the trial?"

"Mr. Samuel?" asked the judge.

"Oh yes, fine," Samuel replied.

"Fine," said the judge, sternly. "I will be leaving to enjoy vacation with my family on August fourteenth, so no delays."

The judge flipped to the next page on the docket before saying authoritatively, "Ms. Morgan, call your next case"—completely unaware that Sandy's life had forever been changed in these last few moments.

CHAPTER 6

SANDY'S SMALL RED CONVERTIBLE TOOK THE CURVES WITH EASE AS she carefully made her way to her parents' Arcadian cabin. Behind her seat was an overnight bag filled with a few items she had thrown together at the last minute when she decided to get out of town for a spell.

In the seat next to her sat evidence of the very reason she felt the need to leave—no, to flee—her home just as the sun had risen on this Saturday morning, several weeks after the arraignments of docket number seventy-six. There, on the passenger seat, sat the small brown cardboard box that held the contents of the case that had come to consume her life the last several weeks.

This is not to say that she had, even for a moment, studied the file. In fact, she hadn't even opened the box. Still, every night she carried the small brown box from her office, and every morning she brought it back with her to work. It had also accompanied her home every weekend since that last day of April when she had first held it.

As she drove along the not so scenic I-10 highway to the cabin, she recalled the first night she had brought the box to her New Orleans home. The brand new file sat in this same box on this same seat as it made its way to Sandy's small home near Audubon Park. Driving down St. Charles Avenue, with the occasional streetcar passing, reminded her of stepping back in time. The stately old Victorian

49

mansions were complete with carriage houses and were located near quaint hotels and fashionable restaurants, the occasional theater, and old streetlights. St. Charles was a street that held incomparable charm. It was busy that evening as people walked from their hotels and homes to enjoy the best dining in the world.

The sun's light was just fading. It was a typical summer evening in New Orleans. The air was heavy and thick with high humidity, yet since the scorching Louisiana sun was taking its evening dive, the heat of the day had passed. With her convertible top down, the soft breeze touched Sandy's face as she drove past the old homes and even older oak trees, which colored her drive. Every day, she looked forward to this drive. Naturally, in order to see the sunset just right, she would have to leave after seven, but she considered it a reward for working late.

Despite the scenery, Sandy was angry as she drove. She was angry because of the flood of memories, which dramatically came to her in broken pieces. She strained her memory and pleaded with herself for more details of what had happened to her.

She could recall his hands and odor most of all. His hands were thick, his nails dirty and mostly chewed up. Black hairs stood on his knuckles and the tops of his hands. She was not sure why she had such specific memories of those hands. Yet, even now, she could almost feel them on her, holding her. They were strong hands, especially when compared to her tiny body.

Someone behind her blew the horn, and she realized that the light had turned green at some point—yet she hadn't moved. *All right, buddy*, she thought as she hit the gas.

Then suddenly, as she pulled back onto the road, she was struck by the distinct recollection of the way he smelled—of stale smoke. She had always hated that smell, but now she remembered why. When he was close to her, his odor was so much stronger. She remembered him being close to her face as he told her over and over again that she must not talk about this. His breath was heavy and thick with the old smoke. He kept reminding her that if she told anyone, her father would be so ashamed to learn that she was such a bad little girl. Her assailant said that he was doing these things to her in order to make her happy and feel like a grown-up. She remembered at one point that she cried out in pain. His response was, "You like that, little one?" Sandy slammed on her brakes.

The memory was too much to bear. She could hear the horns blowing behind her, but she was frozen, panic-stricken. She pulled to the side of the road to let the other cars pass her. She looked around for help, suddenly feeling trapped. She could hardly breathe. Sweat beaded on her face and neck. She thought she might vomit.

Several people on the sidewalk stared at her, but she saw no person or place that looked safe to her. She had nowhere to hide. She felt surrounded by danger. Someone began to walk past her car, looking at her curiously. He was a young man, but still, Sandy frantically searched for safety. She pushed the button that operated her car's convertible top, quickly latched it closed, and rolled up the windows. She sat there for a minute, breathing heavily. Her head pushed against the headrest as she strained to calm herself. Sandy knew that her fear wasn't real, that she wasn't in danger. She scolded herself for panicking. With no explanation for it, she began to feel mad—and defiant. Sandy eased her car back onto the road.

She was angry that she was still allowing him to cause her to panic. She was angry that he had done it again, had raped another little girl. Another little girl? How many little girls? *Shit*, she thought.

She was angry that she was the one assigned to the case, and yet the desire for vengeance raged inside her like a disease. She had brought the file home, determined to collect on a debt that she had been owed for over a decade. She planned to pour herself into the effort and let it encompass her until she finally felt satisfied that she had sealed Gurganus's fate.

So that day, the first day, amid the beauty of the drive home, which she genuinely looked forward to every day, the only thing she could see or think of was that small brown box.

Sandy pulled into her driveway. Maybe it was the slight incline, or maybe it was the sharp right-hand turn, but the box slid across the seat toward her and began to fall to the floor. Sandy reached out her hand to stop it. The second she touched that box, she froze. Her eyes were glued to her hand and the brown thing behind it.

Moments later, she came out of her daze and realized that her hand was still on the box. She pulled her hand away and put it to her chest as if she had touched something hot enough to burn her skin. Her eyes, however, never left the box, as though she expected something to jump out at her any minute. As she stared at it in horror, her tears began to well and fall. Sandy's crying turned to weeping, and then to uncontrollable sobbing.

She had no thoughts during this outburst—just raw emotion. The tears were not just for herself, her pain, her childhood fears, and the injuries she bore. Or, perhaps, somewhere deep in her heart, her heavy tears *were* for all those things. Either way, there were no actual thoughts, just blind emotion. Eventually, she began to settle down and tried to catch her breath.

As she regained her composure, she realized that her eyes had not yet left the box. She became furious with herself. How could she waste such tears? Why? She sat there pouting, staring straight ahead, and refusing even to look at the box.

Defiantly, she wiped her eyes with the back of her hand. Sandy resolved that she would not let the man who had raped her rule her life again. She grabbed the door handle with an aggressive determination. Sandy stepped out of her car and into the moonlit darkness. Her eyes quickly went to her watch, which told her that she had sat in that car for nearly an hour. She sighed and walked to the passenger side to retrieve the physical manifestation of her horrendous obligation.

As she unlocked what seemed like a heavy front door, Sandy paused. Normally, she would have dropped the files on her front table to flip through while she ate a quick dinner or brought them straight to the bedroom to read while she watched TV in bed. Not this file, though; this file was unwelcome. Sandy gave it a quick thought and then placed the box on a sitting bench just inside the foyer. It was there that the box remained until the following Monday. This is also where the box was faithfully returned nightly after she carried it home from the office. Each night, Sandy was convinced that this was the night she would delve into the file.

The small brown box sat alone and untouched for many nights. It was visited only by Sandy's eyes, curious and questioning, when she frequently passed by. Several times, Sandy had actually forced herself to go to the box, once evening opening the lid before closing it tight. Was is fear? Was it anger? It may have been either or both, or perhaps it changed each night. Something, though, made Sandy incapable of opening that box to retrieve its contents—one brand new brown file marked *State of Louisiana v. Bruce Gurganus.*

CHAPTER 7

W HEN SHE WAS ALMOST TO THE CABIN, SANDY'S MIND PICTURED the words as they were written in black ink across the front of the file. As she made her final turn onto the narrow, rock-covered street, she imagined *State of Louisiana v. Bruce Gurganus*. It was easy to see the cabin from the main road, as it sat above the land. But the small street (or long driveway, depending how one looked at it) curved its way past a wooden fence and between two ponds to reach the top of a hill where the cabin sat, beckoning her.

Compared to her small home in the crowded city, the twenty or so acres upon which the cabin sat seemed immense. Her parents had owned this retreat in St. Francisville since she was a child. St. Francisville was a small but quaint town, a little over an hour's drive away from the city of New Orleans, where she had grown up. It was not too far away to reach easily, but it was far enough away to make one feel as if she was out of town.

Sandy's father had given the land as a gift to her mother on the occasion of her parents' tenth wedding anniversary. The opportunity came after her father's first year of true financial success as an attorney.

Its nickname, "the cabin," was a bit misleading. Yes, technically, it was an Arcadian cabin, with its sloping roof and wraparound porch. But it was no small structure; instead, it was rather large and featured every amenity one would want in a modern home. The grounds bore beautiful, old cypress trees draped with Spanish moss, which constantly moved with the breeze. When Sandy was a child, her mother had told her that the Spanish moss only moved when Sandy was there—that it was dancing just for her. To this day, it made her smile when she thought of the two of them sitting on the porch, her mom holding her and whispering such sweet words to her.

Far in a corner was a gathering of magnolia trees so large that the family had hung porch swings from the limbs so they could enjoy the lawn on cool day. It was as if Mother Nature had chosen this land and had carefully sprinkled the trees and a small pond on it so as to make it perfect.

The cabin was close enough to the family's New Orleans home that Sandy spent many childhood weekends and summers exploring its nearby landscape. She had quickly come to love this place when she was still small. She was only nine years old when her family came to own the property. The timing couldn't have been more appropriate. Sandy spent countless hours sitting at the edge of the pond, lost in thought. She knew every tree, every turn in every path, and every dip of each hill.

In fact, Sandy believed that she had a spiritual connection with the land. She knew she was safe here, protected. She had often sought refuge here during times of personal turmoil, such as when she evacuated town because a hurricane was coming; the time she had not been named as homecoming queen; the night she had a big fight with her first love; and the first time she lost a trial.

Sandy's heart had convinced her that it was here, at the cabin, that she could repair the broken pieces of her life resulting from the most current tragedy. This was the case when she reached docket number seventy-six. With only two days left before the hearing, it only made sense that she sought the cabin's help. She could no longer postpone preparing for court.

Lost in thought, Sandy hadn't noticed the gray pickup truck under the carport until she actually pulled her car in next to it. The presence of Old Gray, as it was affectionately nicknamed, could only mean one thing: Sandy's father was apparently going to be joining her.

When she saw Old Gray, she had an instant feeling of relief, knowing that her father was there. Seconds later, though, her relief was replaced by an unsettling feeling in her stomach. Her father had always been able to read her. He knew her in a way that didn't come from the spoken word, but from a raw gut instinct. She knew that it would take a miracle for her to drive away from the cabin as she had come to it: undiscovered.

Sandy hesitantly got out the car. Part of her considered getting back into the car and leaving before her father noticed she was there. This was, of course, not really an option, but more of a fleeting thought. She sighed and paused again before throwing the overnight bag on her shoulder and retrieving the small brown box.

She turned the knob of the cabin's back door, which opened into the great room. When in this room, one was in the heart of the cabin. This one room contained the living room, dining room, and kitchen in one large, open area. Across from the back door sat a wall of glass doors overlooking the lake.

As Sandy pushed her way through the door, she found her father sitting at the table. His eyebrows arched, questioning the sudden disturbance, but then they quickly relaxed when he realized who was at the door. Her father quickly rose, approaching her while saying, "Honey! What a surprise."

Her father stood up from the large wooden table.

A police description of her father, short and direct, would paint him as six feet in height, of average weight, with salt-and-pepper hair and a medium build, and without any remarkable scarring or tattoos. To Sandy, though, who had watched that hair turn from dark brown to its current gray, her father was still the tallest man in the world. He was just Dad.

"Papa Bear! I should have known I'd find you here," Sandy said, smiling. "Am I interrupting your peace?"

"Oh," he said, shaking his head, "now, you know better." He extended his arms. "Let me take that for you." In an instant, she realized that he meant the box—and fear slapped her across the face.

Before she could object, Sandy's father took the box from her hands with one arm while pulling her close to him with the other and giving her a squeeze. He hugged her as he always had. She felt twelve again—and safe.

But Sandy found no real relief in his welcome, as she could not bring her eyes to leave the small brown box. Her father tucked it under his arm as if it were a pillow and began to make his way back to the table. Sandy held her breath.

"What brings you to the cabin, dear? Some rest, I hope." Without waiting for a response, he continued. "What's in this box? It feels empty," he said, shaking it fervently.

Sandy was unable to answer. She was unable to move. She stood horrified as her father placed the box on the chair next to the one he had been sitting on—and then proceeded to open it.

Her mouth opened to speak, but she stood in silence. She wanted to tell him to stop, that there was nothing he needed to see in that box, but no words came out of her mouth. She stood there, mouth and eyes open wide in horror, and said nothing.

"Oh, brought some work home, did ya?" he said after casually flipping open the lid and peaking at the box's contents. Panic kicked Sandy in the gut as she watched.

He smiled and shook his head, closing the box. "Well, I refuse to let you waste your entire weekend working. I insist that you rest. You look tired, and anyway, you need to spend some time with the old man." He walked toward her and hugged her again, smiling as if he were teasing her by calling himself old.

Adopting a more serious tone, he took her by the shoulders and said, "Now, honey, it has just occurred to me that you are still standing in the doorway. There's something about your expression that tells me ..." He paused. "Are you all right?" His eyes searched her face. He had always been able to read her. Did he see something now? She cursed herself for standing there like a fool.

When Sandy was a teenager, she thought that her father was able to read her so well because he was an attorney and possessed special attorney mind-reading skills, a characteristic of all good lawyers. She can remember telling him a lie when she was sixteen. It was a simple one. "I was with Amy, Dad; we just ran a bit late."

"Really?" he had said, his face then bearing the same expression as it did now. His eyes searched her face for clues. "What movie did you see?" As he asked the question, his eyes never left her. He was reading every move, every word, and every flinch.

She had paused and looked away before she began to speak. With that pause, her lie was revealed. Before she could say a word, he shook his head and said, "You're grounded. Now tell me where you really were."

She remembers thinking, *Great, my dad had to be a freakin' trial lawyer.*

It is true that one develops a great skill for reading people when one is a trial attorney. Or perhaps one must have a natural ability to read people in order to be a great trial attorney. Either way, her father was the best. He reminded Sandy of a great poker player. He could read a person's hand just by paying attention to the person's words and body language.

In helping her prepare for her first trial, her father had described the clues she should watch for: the timing of the person's pauses, which words the person chose to inflect, when the person swallowed or sighed, and if the person was perspiring. He said, "Now, Sandy, you have to be ready. They will make one telling move, and you'll have them like a tiger pouncing on its prey!" He was just as excited and nervous as she was.

Sandy, when she was a law student, often went to court to watch her father work. At the time, Thomas Morgan, her father, was the managing partner of a small plaintiff's maritime firm. His primary area of focus was maritime injury. With all the waterways in New Orleans, he was never short of fairly lucrative cases.

Her father loved his profession—and he loved the law. He enjoyed talking ad nauseam about his most recent case, about something funny that happened in court, or about the political gossip about the judges. She had heard him say, ever since she was a child, that a lawyer had an obligation to remember that while he had many cases in his file cabinet, his clients each only had one case. It was imperative that the lawyer get it right.

As Sandy matured and heard more stories about her father's clients, and as she saw him win many awards for his dedication to ethics and his pro bono work, she developed a new appreciation for her father. He became an icon to her, like a rock star to a normal child. She looked up to him, like any young child looks up to a father, but there was something just a little more between the two of them. Something different. Something extraordinary.

In fact, ever since she was a young child, Sandy and her father had held entire conversations while seated across the room from one another, using just their eyes. Their senses of humor were similar, too. They were both individuals to whom other people tended to gravitate. They were both dedicated to the law and to their family. Their bond was as much a friendship as it was a parent–child relationship.

However, the birds were not always singing and the grass wasn't always green in the Morgan home. The two certainly had their disagreements, putting her mother, Rose, in the precarious position of mediator. After all, two personalities as strong as theirs could not pass a day without having a good argument. At least, that's what Sandy's mother would say about them. The two certainly knew each other's faults and each other's hot buttons.

Even then, after the angry moments passed, they would laugh at themselves. Her father would say to her, "Honey, the sooner you recognize that I know you better than you know yourself, the better off you'll be. And the sooner you recognize that I am usually right, the better off we'll all be!"

Now, however, standing near the back door of the cabin, she had come face-to-face with her father. His eyes pierced her, searching for an answer and looking for those subtle clues he had taught her to look for in a witness.

Sandy shrugged. "Oh," she said, taking a deep breath. "Just a lot on my mind with work and everything." She looked away, pretending that something outside had caught her eye.

"Hm," he said, still holding onto her shoulders and looking deep into her face as if he wasn't quite sure he believed her. She looked back, flashing the most sincere expression she could muster.

"Well, honey, this was the path you chose," he said, letting go of her shoulders and moving back to the table.

"Dad," she protested.

"Well, I'm just saying," he began, shrugging his shoulders. "I worked hard to ensure that you wouldn't have to overwork yourself." He took his seat at the table and rested his cheek on one of his hands, shaking his head in feigned disbelief. "Years I spent building that firm, and all for you." He had begun to deliver a familiar speech.

"I know, I know." Sandy dropped her keys on the end table and began making her way to the dinner table to join him. "Dad, you know I'm appreciative, but we've been over this too many times to do it again," Sandy said, referring to an argument the two of them had been having since she had graduated from law school. The argument had begun following the first time Sandy had had the guts to tell her dad that she was not coming to work in his office.

Ever since she could remember, her father had told her, "You're going to be a lawyer one day and work at Daddy's office. Together, we're going to rule the world!" This was a proposition that sounded fantastic to her as a little kid. But in law school, Sandy had worked as a law clerk at her father's office. You could say that the experience had changed her perspective.

Working with her father was not the worst part of the job, although it certainly wasn't always the easiest, either. Many times, she felt as if she were still at home. Her father would pop his head into her cubbyhole and remind her that she could have more space in one of the empty offices, if she preferred, or to remind her to take her vitamins, or to ask if she had dinner plans. One time, he even popped in to criticize an outfit she was wearing.

These things, albeit annoying, were minor when compared to the way in which the other attorneys and law clerks treated her. There are only so many under-the-breath comments and snide remarks one can take before one's pride intervenes and raises the question of whether to stay at the job or leave it and find another. Sandy knew that as the founding partner's daughter, she would never be credited for her own achievements. Even worse, she realized how easy it would be to use her father's good name as a crutch, possibly crippling her own abilities.

After graduation, Sandy had retreated to the cabin for several days before calling her father and asking him to meet her there. She had her entire speech planned out and ready. She sat on the couch and stared at the door. When he finally arrived, Sandy found it hard to speak. Instead of delivering the eloquent speech she had prepared, she blurted out, "Dad, I can't work for you."

"What on earth?" he said, puzzled and caught off guard. He dropped his keys on the end table and looked at her.

"Dad, I need to know that I can do it on my own. I want to know that I can make it, that everything I've learned and done is enough to stand the test of my independence." She paused and, because he was confused, took the opportunity to continue. "I had an interview at the DA's office last week. Please understand."

She might as well have punched him in the gut. His face grimaced. "If you wanted a job with the district attorney's office, I could have made a few calls—saved you the interview," he said, sitting down on the couch and staring into space.

"Dad, that would have defeated my purpose." Sandy dropped to her knees next to him and laid her head in his lap, looking up at him. "I love you, but I needed to know if I could do it," she said quietly. "I needed to know if I could do it on my own."

He sat there with a bit of shock and disappointment remaining on his face. He stared out the far windows. "Daddy, I'm sorry I let you down," she said.

Her father turned to her quickly and looked her dead in the eye. He said, "Let me down? Let *me* down? I'm disappointed for myself because I'll miss you. I know it was my dream, not yours. As for you, I am extremely proud. It's just"—he looked at his feet—"well, I've done it the hard way. I didn't have a choice. Years I spent in the JAG Corps trying to 'find myself,' and all for what? I put in the time so that you could have it easier—so you would have it better." His words were strained as he fought the lump in his throat.

"Dad," she started, sitting opposite him on the couch. "I'm sure about this. I'm really sure. Those years as a military JAG lawyer weren't wasted years. They made you who you are—they tested you. You've told me time and time again that a person can't appreciate ease without having known hardship. This is my way of paying dues. I know I'll be overworked and underpaid, but mainly I'll be tested." She paused, her eyes searching his long face. "Dad, I know you understand. More than everyone, surely you understand."

Her father sighed and smiled. "That's a very good argument, Counselor." Shrugging, he said, "Well, as if there ever was a doubt, that line of reasoning is proof that you really are my daughter!"

The district attorney's office called her the following week to offer her a position. She was elated! The first person she called with the news was her father. He made one last failed attempt to convince her not to leave his firm, then he went on to say how proud of her he was.

When she came into the office on her first day and was introduced to everyone, the human resources director asked her how her father was. "You know my dad?" she asked.

"Oh yes, we go way back," the director said, also remarking that he had enjoyed catching up with him the other day. She shook her head—her dad couldn't resist helping her, after all.

Still, she was appreciative of his 'unwanted' butting in, unasked for though it was. In fact, when he took her out to dinner to celebrate her new job, she toasted him, saying, "To my father. I wanted to get this job on my own, but I am fortunate enough to have a father who cares more about my happiness than about my proving a point."

Her father responded by shaking his head and saying, "Well, I couldn't help myself but to call to see how the interview had gone. As far as whether you could have done it on your own, anyone who knows you also knows the answer to that."

Today, however, was no cause to celebrate. Sandy was asking so many questions about so many things in her life that she wondered if her father hadn't been right all along. He, still sitting at the table, continued to read an article without looking up. She let the heavy air out of her lungs and walked back to the table. Sandy started to pick up the box, but she couldn't manage to lift it. In fact, everything seemed heavy: her chest as she breathed in and out, her legs as they walked to the table. As for her heart, well, it had clearly been broken since that day several weeks ago when she did the arraignment for docket number seventy-six.

Sandy put her hand on her father's shoulders. "Daddy, I really can't have an argument right now."

"We're not arguing, honey," he said without looking up.

Seconds later, when Sandy hadn't moved, he gazed up at her. He could see it on her face. Exactly what he was seeing, he wasn't sure, but he did know that she needed something from him and that he had led their conversation in the wrong direction.

"You know what we need?" he asked, putting his hand over top her hand. "A special batch of my lick," he answered himself with enthusiasm.

Lick was a desert that had been passed down in their family for an unknown number of generations. The ingredients were simple: cocoa, sugar, and milk. Warm until boiling, then serve on a flat plate. The result was, for all practical purposes, fudge before it had hardened. Its name came from the fact that as kids, they would dip their fingers in the still-warm chocolate and then lick it off.

Sandy smiled despite her bad mood as her father made his way to the stove and began making the concoction. She pulled out a bar stool and sat down.

"Where's Mom?" she asked, happy to have changed the subject and tempo of their conversation.

"Oh, she had a speeding ticket and I asked the judge to give her five years," he responded without even looking at her or laughing.

"Dad," she half protested, rolling her eyes.

"What?" he said, exaggerating a shoulder shrug. "He owed me a favor."

Sandy smiled despite herself. She looked over her shoulder at the box patiently waiting for her on the table, then back at her father. Sighing heavily, she gave in.

Several hours later, their having enjoyed lick together and then a pizza by the lake, the two retired to the porch swing for iced tea and some much-needed, relaxing conversation. Dusk eventually began to descend. The scene was picturesque with the dark orange glimmer of the sun barely touching the edge of the lake. A faint breeze floated across their faces like butterfly kisses from a child. The soft croaking of what Sandy affectionately called the invisible frogs was audible.

Sandy and her father had spent many evenings this way. When she was a child, they would sit on this same swing and listen to the deep croaking song of the frogs.

"I can't see them, Daddy," Sandy would complain.

Her father would reassure her. "They're there, honey. Don't they always come to sing the sun a good-night lullaby?"

"Well, I can't see them. And anyway, lullabies are sweet, not frog noises," Sandy would retort.

The two would continue the argument or sometimes laugh when they imagined which family member the frogs sounded like when they sang. Either way, Sandy never could see the "invisible frogs," but ultimately she came to understand that a person can't always see what is really there, right in front of her.

This night, though, Sandy's eyes didn't search for the elusive frogs, since she chose instead to sit comfortably next to her father and simply enjoy the frogs' song. It was too soon that the two picked up their glasses to make their way back inside the cabin. As they walked in, Sandy sighed heavily once she saw the small brown box still waiting for her at the table. Her father said, "Hey, how about a hot bubble bath while I put on some tea—that file will be waiting tomorrow."

Sandy looked at him, then back to the box. "I don't know, Dad. I should get started."

"No worries—we'll get through it in the morning. Together," he said reassuringly.

Sandy shook her head, her soft brown hair brushing each shoulder, her eyebrows and mouth scowling. "I may need to go this one alone, Dad. See, it's an ... important case," she said slowly.

"Aren't they all, honey?" he responded gently.

CHAPTER 8

WEARING HER OLD TERRY CLOTH ROBE AND OVERSIZED SLIPPERS, she sat at the table alone. Her hair had been pulled neatly back the night before, but now many of her soft brown locks had made their way out of the barrette and found themselves resting around her forehead and shoulders. She drank from a mug bearing the logo of the local sheriff's department. Over time, it had faded.

It had taken her nearly an hour to get to this point. She had finally given up on trying to sleep a little after 5:00 a.m. After making a pot of coffee, she had sat down at the table next to the brown box. She dreaded touching it.

The coffee was ready. She drank a cup at the bar in the kitchen, staring across the open room to the box on the chair. She poured another cup, sipping from it while she paced next to the table, glancing occasionally at her nemesis. After pouring her third cup, she forced herself to walk to the table and open the top of the box. *Don't think about it*, she chastised herself. *You are being ridiculous.*

Sandy reached in, took out the file, and, with two fingers, flipped open the cover. After staring at a page for a couple of seconds, she sat down at the table. She took long, deep drinks of her coffee as her eyes read carefully over the first page of the file, which sat open on the table just past her coffee cup.

Both of her hands were wrapped around the cup as if it held the last bit of water on Earth. Although she had already read the first page several times, she had failed to comprehend a single word. Each time she read it, she would tell herself, *This time I will pay attention. Focus. Focus,* she demanded of herself.

This first page of the file was titled "Bill of Information" and bore basic information about the case: the defendant's name and birthdate, the case number, etc. The purpose of the bill of information was to specifically outline the charges against the defendant.

The bill read, in part:

> On or about the 23rd day of February, the defendant, Bruce Gurganus, did commit the following illegal acts:
>
> Count One: sexual assault of a minor, namely Adorina Dauzat, age five.
>
> Count Two: carnal knowledge of a juvenile, namely Adorina Dauzat, age five.
>
> Count Three: forcible rape of a juvenile, namely Adorina Dauzat, age five.

Sandy paused. Her mind was blank. *Did I just read that again?* she wondered. *What did it say?* She sighed as she stood up to pour a fresh cup of coffee. She sat back down and pulled a legal pad from her briefcase. *All right,* she thought, *now I'm ready.* She read the charges again.

> Count One: sexual assault of a minor, namely Adorina Dauzat, age five.
>
> Count Two: carnal knowledge of a juvenile, namely Adorina Dauzat, age five.

> Count Three: forcible rape of a juvenile, namely
> Adorina Dauzat, age five.

She stared blankly at the page, as if she had just read a confusing chemistry article. *Turn the page,* she thought. Her hands refused to cooperate. "Turn the page," she said sternly to herself. She turned her head to look out the window.

I need to concentrate, she thought, as she watched two birds hop along the porch rail. *Gee, it's sunny today. … Concentrate!* She moved her eyes back to the open file. The bill of information was still staring back, taunting her.

"It's six-thirty, honey," her father said quietly as if someone in the cabin was still asleep. Sandy looked up to find his familiar slow-moving, stiff frame making its way from his bedroom.

He had a hard time bending his knees in the morning, which seemed to be worsening with age. He attributed the stiffness to his years in the army. Sandy and her mother would tease her father about his "old military wounds."

"Yeah, Dad, that JAG office sure was dangerous. No, it's not arthritis in your knees, it's all those years of fighting the other pencil pushers in the JAG office that did you in!"

Her father would shake his head, smiling. "Smarty-pants," he would say. "I did go through basic training, you know. Our enemies are just lucky it was peacetime, that's all!" her father would tease back.

Sandy jumped slightly at the sound of his voice. "Did I wake you?" she asked, relieved to have an excuse to look at anything other than the file.

"Nah," he said, pulling his robe around himself and making a beeline to the coffeepot. "This familiar smell was my alarm clock," he said, nodding his head affectionately at the coffeepot. "Why are you up so early? Didn't you sleep comfortably?"

"Not really. A lot on my mind, I guess," Sandy replied dryly as her father placed the glass pot back into its cradle before his feet padded toward her.

He put his steaming coffee cup on the table before making his way to the front door and disappearing out of it. Moments later, he returned to the cabin and his seat at the table with the newspaper tucked safely under his arm. He had not changed this routine much since Sandy was a child.

Opening the newspaper and settling in for his morning caffeine fix, he started reading about the latest tragedies and events. Her father hadn't noticed that the newspaper covered part of Sandy's file. "So, what's so bothersome about this case that you can't sleep?" he asked, not taking his eyes away from his paper as he sipped his coffee and flipped the page.

Sandy huffed in aggravation. His eyes moved to her face. She raised her eyebrows and gave an exaggerated nod to indicate that his paper was on top of her file. "Sorry, honey," he said, although his tone indicated that he wasn't really sorry. Then, looking back at his paper, he continued speaking. "It's just that I couldn't help but notice that in the five minutes I've been awake, you haven't yet turned the page. And call me crazy, but isn't that the very first page? Half a pot of coffee and you are on the first page?" His eyes returned to her quickly, searching to get a read on her response.

Sandy just continued to stare blankly at his face before her eyes started to dart around the first page, looking for an explanation. What could she say? The page was too long ... too complicated ... too what? Her father put down the paper and demanded, "What is it, for crying out loud?"

Sandy knew that she needed to provide some explanation. To simply say it was a tough case wouldn't pacify her father at this point. Then it occurred to her to tell the truth—sort of.

"It's a child rape case," she said flatly. There. Now that it was out, maybe he would let it go.

"Oh," he said quietly, as if he were trying to think of what to say next. "Well, what are the facts?"

"Dad," Sandy exclaimed, not trying to hide the fact that she didn't want to talk about it. *This is none of his business,* she thought. *He knows nothing of criminal law. He has no idea.*

"Come now," he said, a little defensively. "I'm a grown-up. I can handle it. What are the facts of the case?"

Typical, Sandy thought; *he's not going to let me out of this.* She opened her mouth to begin reciting the facts when she realized that she wasn't really sure what they were. "I haven't been able to get past the first page, the bill of information. All I really know are the charges against the defendant."

Her father folded the newspaper and placed his glasses on top of it, then stared at her blankly. "I thought you said the hearing was tomorrow," he said, folding his hands on the table in front of himself.

She resigned herself to hearing what she was sure would be a scolding about her obligation to the victim and what it takes to be adequately prepared. She looked back at him. He sat staring at her, waiting for a response.

"Yes, the hearing is tomorrow," she said in an embarrassed whisper.

Her father watched her for a moment. Perhaps it was the pitiful look on her face, or perhaps it was the fact that he knew she wasn't sleeping well. Whatever the case may be, he did not scold her. Her father sighed, carefully set his paper on the far end of the table, and put his hand on hers. "Where should we begin?"

Sandy looked away. Her mind raced. She was reluctant to let her father help. The fear of that alone was part of what had kept her up the previous night. She was afraid that he would recognize the defendant's name, or that the case would remind him of what had happened to her, or that a hundred other things would go wrong.

As she tossed the idea around, though, she took comfort in two facts. The first was that she herself did not recognize Gurganus's name when she first saw it, and the second was that her father had picked up the file the day before and hadn't given any indication that he recognized the defendant's name.

She looked at her father. He was looking right back. She thought, *I'll just pretend that this is like any other case. I can do this. I can do this.*

"Well, tomorrow is only the motions hearing." Her father's eyebrows knitted, showing that he was curious. "The only two motions pending are"—Sandy finally flipped the paper over to review the next page before continuing—"a motion to withdraw the jury request and...," Sandy flipped the page again, "a motion in limine." She glanced at her father, whose face still wore an expression of thoughtfulness. She continued. "A motion in limine is," she started before her father interrupted.

"A motion to limit!" he exclaimed. "For crying out loud, I've practiced law for over thirty years, not to mention that I speak Latin. I mean, I'm sure I know what a motion in limine is!" he said, shaking his head and rolling his eyes. Then he gave a small chuckle. "What, my dear, are they trying to limit?"

Sandy smiled. "Well, I was just making sure you were on top of your game, old-timer! Didn't know if they taught that way back when." Sandy laughed at herself. "Let's see," she continued as she read the page for the first time, "they are trying to exclude the fingerprint evidence, the defendant's statement, the forensic tests performed on the duct tape found wrapped around the victim's wrists and across her mouth, and the DNA test performed on the defendant, which matched semen found on the child's body."

"Okay," said her father, "before we go through each of those, tell me what the deal with the first motion is. How can you dismiss a jury that you haven't even selected yet?"

"Oh, didn't learn that one in Latin class, Papa Bear?" she teased.

"Help an old civil lawyer out, would you!" he replied, smiling.

"The gist of the motion is that they are asking for a judge trial rather than a jury trial." Her father nodded as she continued. "It's basically the defendant's right to have a jury trial, but it is not a requirement." Sandy thought for a moment. "Did I tell you who the defense attorney is?" she asked.

"No."

"Well, the defense attorney is a real piece of work. His name is Robert Samuel, but the judge just calls him Bob," she said, making imaginary quotation marks in the air. "They act like old buddies."

"Well, the judge should be recused if there is any impropriety," her father started.

Sandy interrupted him by saying, "Nah, you know how these things go, Dad. You can't make those kind of waves without losing your job. And anyway, this judge has always come across as pretty fair." Sandy shrugged. "Anyhow, this motion, the motion to excuse the jury, is a freebie for the defense—and it's nearly always granted. It's the second motion that is the real meat of the motions hearing."

"Oh, okay. Fine. Let's take the items he seeks to exclude one by one and prepare our arguments about why Bob is absolutely wrong," her father said with clear determination in his voice.

Sandy carefully balanced herself on the chair, tucking her feet under her bottom and getting more comfortable for the first time since she woke up that morning.

"You know, these motions in limine are one of the standard defense motions that we usually win," Sandy explained. "Judges like to leave the evidence to the jury. Sometimes, I think defense attorneys only file these so they can convince their clients that it was worth the umpteen thousands they paid to be represented," Sandy said sardonically. "Truthfully, I don't usually spend much time on these. My arguments are pretty standard, unless the cops screwed things up by improperly collecting the evidence."

Sandy looked back at the file for a second before realizing that her father hadn't responded. She lifted her head to find him staring at her with curiosity.

"What?" she said.

Her father didn't reply right away but took a second to phrase his questions so that they sounded just right. "So, why is this case different? Why the sleepless night? Why the extra preparation?"

They were good questions. Even though he had caught her off guard, she answered her father without much forethought. She looked him straight in the eye and said honestly, "I just can't let this guy go, Dad. I can't let him walk out of that courtroom free to rape a child again."

Her father drew a deep breath before saying, "I understand." He nodded and, with a genuine smile, said, "I get it. I do. Now, let's get to the evidence."

And with that, Sandy and her father began their work.

Sandy chose to start with the initial police report. While this type of report is a great tool for providing one with an overall understanding of the facts of the case, it had been Sandy's experience that police reports weren't completely reliable. It seems that sometimes people gave statements to the reporting officer, who either heard it wrong or wrote it down wrong. Inevitably, when she'd interview the witness, the story would be different. Sometimes the differences were minor, and then sometimes the witness' story was so different that it changed the entirety of the case.

In cases such as the one she was now working on, the reporting officer completed the initial police report, and a detective later filed a supplemental report. It is usually the supplemental report that contains the facts of the investigation—those that led to a defendant's arrest.

In looking at the initial police report, Sandy found some of the unquestionable, hard facts. The police were called to the scene at 11:42 p.m. The caller was Lee Lawson, who had dialed 9-1-1 for an ambulance when he found the minor child, whom he called Dori Dauzat, crying in the backyard. She appeared to be bleeding, but he couldn't determine from where. When asked if he needed police assistance, he replied, "I'm not sure. I don't understand what is going on here."

The 9-1-1 operator called for the ambulance and also the police. The reporting officer, Seth Tyler, was the first to arrive on the scene, just seconds before the ambulance. Mr. Lawson refused the paramedics access to the child and refused when they tried to take the child into custody.

In the report, Mr. Lawson was described as a close friend of the family who was babysitting the child that night. He did not have proper written authorization to admit the child to the hospital. The child was Adorina Dauzat, born the twelfth day of December, age five. She was clothed in a white nightgown, ankle-length and with long sleeves to the wrists. The gown showed several red markings of what appeared to be blood. The child had blood on her face and hands and in her long blonde hair.

According to the police report, the child refused to speak and only cried uncontrollably. Mr. Lawson informed them that he had found the child in the backyard crying, with her wrists bound together by gray duct tape. Her mouth had been taped closed with another piece of that tape.

Mr. Lawson told the police that the child's parents were attending a Mardi Gras ball at the Superdome, where Adorina's father was being honored as a float lieutenant of the krewe. Mr. Lawson provided the police with two cellular phone numbers: one for the child's mother and the other for the child's father. Neither phone had service at the time of the incident.

When the ambulance had arrived at the Lawson home, a detective aided in convincing Mr. Lawson to give the child to the paramedics so that they may attend to her. Interestingly, the report specifically spoke of the child's reaction. Adorina screamed a deep, fearful scream, which, to the officer, seemed to last for hours. She reached for Mr. Lawson and continued to scream for him. The same police officer accompanied the child to the hospital.

After mentioning a preliminary discussion with the doctor, the initial police report ended with the determination that the child had sustained a sexual assault. A detective from the child abuse unit of the NOPD had already been assigned to the case and called to the scene.

Detective Bradley Curtis arrived at the home before the ambulance had taken the child. He eventually detained Lee Lawson for questioning. Another police officer was sent to the Superdome to locate and inform the child's parents.

Sandy finished reading from the short initial police report and looked at her father. He looked concerned. "Don't worry, the meat of our case is usually found in the supplemental police report and the forensic evidence," she said, smiling at him.

He responded curtly, "You'd better hope so."

Sandy pulled the supplemental report from the file and leaned back in her chair, smiling faintly when she saw the handwriting she knew well. Sandy and Bradley Curtis had worked close together on a stalking-cum-attempted-homicide case a few weeks earlier. She had only seen him a few times since his promotion to the child abuse unit.

"What's the joke?" her father asked when he saw her grin.

"Oh, no, it's nothing. It's just … I know this detective, that's all," she said, coming back to reality.

"I see." He leaned toward her, curious. "How well?" her father asked, a smile starting to float across his face.

"Not that well, Dad!" she exclaimed, rolling her eyes and shrugging away his suggestion. "We just worked together once. No big deal. I just know when I see his name that it's a sound report and that he's a strong witness," she said, shaking her head. She stole a look at her father, whose eyebrows were raised and whose smile was growing. "Okay," she continued with a flash of red coloring her cheeks, "we had dinner once, as part of a group, but only to celebrate the victory—that's all!"

Her father crossed his arms and looked at her, waiting patiently.

"Fine, we've gone to a movie, and we had coffee together twice. But it's no big deal. He's not even my type at all. Stop smiling at me like that; I'm serious!" Sandy was grinning as she swatted at her father's arm.

He uncrossed his arms and picked up the page he had left off at. Under his breath, as if he didn't mean for Sandy to hear him, he said, "You know, over thirty years ago I married the last girl I dated who wasn't my type."

She shrugged off the smile as she carefully began to read the supplemental report. She took careful notes as she read, then passed each page to her father when she had finished with it. That, paired with several calls to the handsome detective, during which he recounted the case, helped her slowly piece things together.

Detective Bradley Curtis started his supplemental report as he always did, with the history of the victim. Then he carefully chronicled every move he made during his investigation. He noted his personal observations of his initial suspect, mentioned that the DNA on the child's undergarments and nightgown matched Bruce Gurganus's, noted that the fingerprints found on the tape matched Bruce Gurganus's, and mentioned that the child had identified Bruce Gurganus, from a mug shot, as her attacker.

Sandy carefully read each page, taking notes on her yellow legal pad. At one point, as she handed the next page to her father to read, she noticed that he, too, was carefully reading each page and was making a list of notes. Sandy smiled at their similarities.

When she was done, she got up to make them sandwiches while her father finished up. They had been sitting there for hours, neither one of them moving. The coffee had gone cold and morning had passed to early afternoon. It wasn't until Sandy stood up and stretched that she realized just how long they had been there. She was hungry and ready to be distracted.

She brought the sandwiches to the table just as her dad put his pen down.

"Whew. Honey, is this what you deal with all the time?"

"Well, yeah, Dad, I guess it is. I mean, most cases aren't this hideous. But, sure, I deal with the ugly side of the law."

Her dad pulled his sandwich toward himself. "Thanks, hon," he muttered.

"So, what do you think? I feel better having read everything. I mean, with the DNA and fingerprints, it should be a pretty open-and-shut case," Sandy said. She bit into her turkey sandwich.

"Yes, the man practically left you a note with his address on it," her father replied. "So, what is the point of going through motions hearings and ultimately a trial? I would just try to negotiate for as little time as possible—you know, beg for leniency."

Sandy nodded. "I know—me, too! I guess this is going to trial for the same reason they all do: because the perpetrators deny having committed the crime. It amazes me sometimes."

They both sat a moment munching their sandwiches and lost in thought. Finally, her father said, "You know, one major thing bothers me." He paused and cocked his head to the side. "How did the attacker know that the child was at Lawson's that night?"

"What do you mean?" asked Sandy.

"The rapist. How did he know that Dori was there? Lawson doesn't have kids, and he wouldn't really have a reason to have a kid there on that particular night. So, how did the perp know that she was there?" Her father put down his sandwich and looked at her questioningly.

Sandy put her sandwich down, too. Looking at her father, she arched her eyebrows questioningly as well. After several minutes, she answered him honestly. "You know, I have no idea."

CHAPTER 9

THERE'S ALWAYS ONE PIECE, SANDY COMPLAINED TO HERSELF AS SHE pulled her hair back in a tight ponytail at the base of her neck. As she fastened the barrette, several strands of hair fell to the side of her face, eluding the binding clip. *To hell with it,* she thought as she tucked the aggravating hair behind her right ear. She didn't have time to fuss with such minute details.

Today was the day: the motions hearing.

She had spent the weekend sleeping with the enemy. Literally. Sandy and her dad had spent hours poring over the information contained in the file, sharing Chinese takeout and pot after pot of coffee. Then last night, Sunday, Sandy relaxed as she made the long drive home from the cabin. When she got home, she made a fresh pot of coffee and snuggled in her bed. The only noise was the soft sound of her favorite country station humming so low that it was barely audible. Comfortable, she opened the file and read until she fell asleep with her notes for today's arguments.

She was ready. Donning her favorite red power suit and black stilettos, she nodded approvingly at herself in the mirror before walking out the front door. In fact, she practically pranced out of the house to make the short drive to the courthouse. *Hm, perfect weather to serve up a little justice,* she thought confidently.

Sandy smiled and turned the radio up when she realized that traffic was much lighter than usual. *Yep,* she thought, *it's a sign!* Sandy wasn't really what you'd call a superstitious person—or, at least, she would deny that she was. But if you watched her close enough, you would hear her talk about signs or luck, or catch her knocking on the occasional piece of wood to prevent being jinxed.

She turned into the near-empty parking lot of the district attorney's office, yanked the rolling cart of files out of her trunk, and headed into the courthouse across the street. She noticed what a nice Monday morning it was, indeed!

She used her hips to swing open the courtroom door and pull her rolling files through. Once inside, she organized the files for the day's pretrial hearings, twelve in total, and then took her seat at the prosecution's table. She reached into her briefcase and pulled out a brand new legal pad. She placed it on the table, reached back into her briefcase, and grabbed her favorite blue ink pen. She zipped her briefcase closed, tucked it next to the table, pulled her chair in to rest under the table, and sat up straight in her chair—pen ready to take notes.

The silence in the courtroom finally struck her. It was 8:12 a.m. Court started at nine.

Funny, she thought, *I'm never this early.*

And there she sat. Waiting.

Eventually, the courtroom began to fill—first with a couple people, who seemed nervous to have arrived early and quietly found seats in the back row. Then, slowly, the room began to hum softly with voices. Eventually, the courtroom filled with the lively conversation of attorneys, the quiet, desperate conversations of their clients, and the occasionally off-color joke of a bailiff.

Sandy had long since lost the quiet morning. It had been replaced with her normal activities—answering questions, making plea offers, and jotting down consent agreements.

As was their usual routine, the two bailiffs with the sheriff's department led in that day's group of prisoners. The prisoners were wearing the usual: wrinkled orange uniforms. Out of the corner of her eye, Sandy could see them enter the room. They casually took their seats on the far side. Sandy busied herself with her files so as not to accidentally make eye contact with the orange-suited defendants.

As if on cue, a stern voice with a heavy Southern accent captured her attention from several feet behind her.

"Ms. Sandra Morgan," it said.

Sandy took a brief moment to weigh her options for evasion before silently conceding that she had none. She turned around to face the enemy. "Mr. Robert Samuel," she said, mustering a smile and extending her hand for the usual gentleman's handshake.

"So lovely to see you, dear," he responded, taking her hand and turning it gently to the side, palm down. Samuel began lifting her hand to his mouth, which proudly displayed a neatly trimmed mustache and a cunning smile.

This isn't a social call, you idiot, she thought as she sharply pulled her hand from his before one hair of that mustache touched her skin. "We only have twelve on the docket today. I took the liberty of making sure your case goes first," she told him.

"Yes, yes. That was very kind of you. The quicker I finish here, the sooner I make it to my office, and you know what that means?" Samuel asked rhetorically while he smiled and tugged on his pressed white sleeves to ensure that his diamond cuff links were showing.

"Actually," Sandy replied dryly, "I have no idea what that means."

Samuel rocked on his heels and chuckled. "Why, the sooner I get to my office, the sooner I get to bill the next client, child."

Sandy couldn't hide the look of disgust that crept across her face. Her eyebrows crinkled.

"Of course," she muttered sardonically.

From across the room, the bailiff's voice sounded the court's version of good morning: "All rise!"

The judge, wearing his long black robe, came in through the door, climbed the couple steps to his desk on the bench, and plopped down into his seat.

"The Honorable Judge Bryson presiding. God bless this court, and God bless the state of Louisiana. You may be seated," the bailiff said authoritatively.

The courtroom filled with the sounds of shuffling and soft whispers.

"Good morning," the judge said cheerfully, grabbing a copy of the docket and removing the top from his pen. "All right, let's see, number one on the docket, State versus Gurganus. Counselors, make your appearances."

"Sandra Morgan on behalf of the State of Louisiana."

"Robert Samuel on behalf of Mr. Gurganus, Your Honor. We are here today, Judge, on behalf of the defendant's motion to withdraw the jury request and his motion in limine."

"These are both the defendant's motions?" the judge asked, flipping through the file and regretting not having read them the night before.

"Yes, Judge Bryson. May I proceed?" asked Samuel.

"Please do," replied the judge, skimming the page.

"May it please the court," began Samuel. "After much discussion with my client, I discerned that he has thoughtfully considered his predicament. While he feels that he is clearly innocent and that a jury would surely find him so, he has decided to withdraw his request for a jury and let his fate rest solely in Your Honor's hands."

Sandy opened her mouth to speak, but Samuel continued.

"The truth is, Judge, your reputation for being a fair, honest, and noble judge precedes you," Samuel continued.

Sandy thought his approach cunning. *Here we go,* she said to herself.

"Wanting not to waste the court's valuable time—nor the tax dollars of the great citizens of our parish—on what will surely prove to be a case with insufficient evidence against poor Mr. Gurganus, who is left to defend himself against such brutal charges, he has decided to withdraw his jury request." Samuel finished, his hand now resting soothingly on his client's shoulders.

"State?" asked the judge, looking up from the file only to pass a grin to Mr. Samuel.

Although she wanted to respond with a comment about how uncomfortable the judge must be, sitting there with Samuel's lips pressed against his backside, she replied simply, "No objection."

"Fine," began the judge, "it's so ordered. What else?"

"Wonderful, Your Honor," said Samuel, patting his client on the back and nodding at him as if it was his argument that had caused the judge to render the order and as if he had been awarded some kind of prize.

Idiot, thought Sandy, *this is always granted. It's one's right, for crying out loud.*

"Finally, Judge, you will find there in that file our motion in limine. My client is in the unfortunate position of asking that the fingerprint evidence found at the home, the forensic DNA evidence found on the tape found wrapped around this poor child's wrists and across her mouth, as well as the forensic DNA evidence of semen found on the child's person and clothes, be removed from the State's permissible evidence, as this evidence is no longer available for the defendant to have it independently tested."

Both the judge and Sandy stared at him with their eyebrows arched.

"Judge," Sandy began before the judge interrupted her.

"There, there. Let's take these individually. First, let's address the fingerprint evidence."

"Why, of course, Your Honor," began Samuel. "My client is specifically requesting that this evidence be excluded because Mr. Gurganus had done some work on that home and has every reason for his fingerprints to be on the tape."

"A point I am sure he will bring up during the trial, Judge," said Sandy. "That is no reason to keep the fingerprint evidence out."

"Actually, Judge, I strongly disagree with this young lady. As the court is aware, I have been trying criminal cases for three decades. It is clear to me that such evidence is highly prejudicial and has no place in the record," argued Samuel.

"'Young lady!' I'm an officer of the court," Sandy protested.

"All right, all right," said the judge, motioning with his hands for the two of them to be quiet. "Mr. Samuel, you will have every opportunity at trial to demonstrate why your client's fingerprints were found, wherever they were found, and to question the technique and mechanism by which they were used to identify your client. I'm going to deny your motion, as it relates to the prints. What's next, the DNA?"

"Please note my objection for the record," Samuel said, winking at his client as if he had hoped that this would be the judge's ruling.

"Duly noted. Please continue."

"Next, Your Honor, it disheartens me to make the following request, but after much discussion with the crime lab, it appears to me that the DNA that was collected at the scene on that dark evening has been misplaced. Mr. Gurganus desperately needs that evidence in order to independently test it," he continued, dramatically pointing his finger at Sandy and raising his tone, "as I am certain that it will disprove any connection he is accused of having to this tragedy!"

"Your Honor," began Sandy, exacerbated, "the State is unaware of any such misplacement of evidence. This is outrageous. I have not had the opportunity to speak with anyone from the crime lab to verify this. Mr. Samuel should be reprimanded and sanctioned for failing to disclose this information so that I may have had the opportunity to investigate the allegation." Sandy spoke faster and faster, her mind racing, her mouth spitting out any idea, hoping that at least one of her arguments would catch the judge's attention.

"With all due respect to the State and its opportunities," Samuel interrupted, making quotation marks in the air with two fingers of each hand as he said the word *opportunities*, "but poor Mr. Gurganus lies in wait as his life is held hostage under these brutal and untrue allegations." He flailed his arms to overexaggerate the importance of each sentence.

Sandy couldn't hide her outrage. She turned to face Samuel directly. "This is ridiculous. Did you see the evidence against your 'poor' client?"

The crack of the wooden gavel startled her.

"Enough, really," said the judge as he set down the file and rubbed his eyes. "The two of you, really, this is not a stage. It is a courtroom. Enough with all the fussing, or you'll both be writing me checks for your sanctions."

The judge paused before shrugging his shoulders. "Mr. Samuel, I see in the record that of the samples collected, there was DNA extracted from eleven of them. Is it your understanding that all eleven are lost?"

"That's correct, Judge. All eleven of the only evidence that can exculpate my client has been lost," responded Samuel, insisting on turning the issue to his client's benefit.

There was a second of silence before Sandy saw her opportunity. "Your Honor," she began, "this evidence has been thoroughly tested. The DNA clearly demonstrates that Mr. Gurganus was not only there, but that at some point he excreted semen onto the child and her gown. This evidence is vital to our case. The defense will have every opportunity to challenge our expert under cross-examination ..."

The judge interrupted her. "I hear you, Ms. Morgan. I do. The problem is that the defense has the right to hire its own expert. If there is nothing to test, we can't just default to the State's expert. If that is how we operated, then evidence would get lost all the time. Your expert can't be rewarded for carelessness."

"Your Honor," started Sandy, taking a few steps closer to the judge in desperation, "the problem is that I don't know that the evidence has been lost. I have had no correspondence or update from the crime lab or Mr. Samuel until this moment. I would ask that this hearing be reset, giving us thirty days to resolve this question."

"Your Honor, I object to the callous request made by my young colleague. The State has had ample time to retrieve and relinquish such evidence." By this time, Samuel had moved closer to the judge as well. Both attorneys were standing nearly at the base of his elevated desk.

"All right. Enough. I am ready to make my ruling. The motion is stayed until seven days from today. The State has seven days to produce for testing the requested items. Should the evidence not be made available within seven days, then the motion is granted, as it relates to the DNA evidence. The ruling on the fingerprints stands." With this, the judge flipped over the file and began reaching for the next one—just as Sandy began her objection.

"But, Your Honor, seven days? I don't...," she nearly whimpered.

"That's my ruling, Ms. Morgan. You have the right to disagree. It is called the Fourth Circuit Court of Appeal. Call your next case."

Sandy stood, blinking back her shock, before she turned to walk to her desk, feeling defeated. She moved in just enough time to see Samuel shaking the hand of a monster. Both men were smiling.

Her sense of defeat was quickly replaced with anger—deep-rooted anger that made her face feel warm and her hands shake.

CHAPTER 10

It was simply a matter of bad timing.

Sandy is standing on the sidewalk. Across the street, then across the median, on the opposite street, she sees him. He stands on the corner of the ice cream shop, leaning against the building and taking long drags of his cigarette.

She just stands there, watching him. She can feel that something bad is going to happen. The streetcar pulls up and screeches to a stop right in front of her, blocking her view of him. Lee Lawson jumps out from the door in the far rear. He is smiling. He turns and picks up the little girl in her bright pink dress and lifts her high before playfully putting her on the ground. It's Dori.

The two hold hands and begin walking behind the streetcar, disappearing on the other side.

Oh no. Sandy's heart rate speeds up. Without thinking, she begins crossing the street to reach the median. She makes it across and onto the grass as the streetcar begins to move forward.

She waits for it to pass, the movement causing the warm summer wind to blow across her face. It passes, and her eyes dart to the corner where he had stood waiting. He's gone.

Her eyes float across the front of the building, searching. Then Dori bounces out of the ice cream shop, laughing and licking a cone.

She and Lee are holding hands. In the distance, she sees smoke. Dori and Lee turn the corner toward the smoke.

Sandy panics. She walks across the median, gaining speed with each step. She sees him step out behind Dori and Lee as they pass him. He turns and looks at Sandy, smiling.

Sandy starts running, darting into the street. A car's brakes squeal as she is nearly hit. She turns her head to look at the car as it is coming toward her. The horn blows loudly as she braces for the blow.

Sandy sits upright in her bed. She looks around frantically, trying to get her bearings. Her chest moves up and down, her nightgown wet from sweat. She looks at the clock; it's just after three in the morning.

Another nightmare. She is averaging three a week.

She takes a long drink of water from the cup on her nightstand.

I have to stop this, she scolds herself.

CHAPTER 11

"ONE MORE DAY, DETECTIVE, ONE MORE DAY!" SANDY PRACTICALLY shrieked into the phone.

"Detective? Oh, now I'm 'Detective,'" said the deep voice on the other end.

"Exactly what is that supposed to mean?" Sandy demanded, indignant.

"Wasn't it just last week when I asked you to dinner? I was Bradley then. Now I'm Detective?"

Sandy paused for a minute to regain her composure. Determined not to change the direction of the conversation, she said more calmly, "You know, I have invested so much in this case. I just don't want him to get away because *your* crime lab lost the most important evidence we have."

Detective Bradley Curtis chuckled. "Wow. *My* crime lab. Is that right? Well, maybe you can pin me with that Kennedy assassination if you stretch this any further. You've done this long enough to know that I don't even work in the crime lab."

Sandy sighed heavily. Then, in a soft tone, she said, "Bradley, I just don't know what to do."

There was a short pause as Curtis, weakened by her tone, thought of a response. "I'll tell you what," Curtis began, his voice softening, "I will check one more time. I will personally walk through every inch of that lab. If it is there to be found, I will find it. Okay?"

Sandy shrugged her shoulders and plopped back down into her office chair. She turned to face the large windows. In the distance, she could see the police station on the other side of the courthouse. "Okay," she relented.

"There is a condition, of course," he said.

"Naturally," Sandy said sarcastically, rolling her eyes and smiling despite herself.

"Dinner. You said you were busy. I think maybe you should unbusy yourself."

Sandy sighed, faking reluctance. "Fine, I'll even buy," she said at last. "But get me my evidence first."

She hung up the phone without saying good-bye, smiling with the hope that her Boy Scout would pull through for her.

Seconds later, the button on her phone blinked red, indicating that a call was on hold. Sandy picked up the receiver, and two things happened simultaneously. First, Sandy said, "Missed me already?"

As the word *already* was coming out of her mouth, Tony, Sandy's paralegal, burst through the door and said, "Don't answer!"

On the other line, the deep Southern growl of Robert Samuel answered her question with, "Why, indeed I did!"

Sandy looked at Tony, horrified. He shrugged his shoulders in an "I told you so" sort of way and then walked out the door, closing it behind himself.

"I thought you were someone else, Mr. Samuel," Sandy said dryly.

"My, my, my. And a lucky someone he is," he responded.

"Can I help you with anything, or is this a social call?" Sandy asked.

"Well, I suppose it could have been social, but your change in tone tells me that I should just get to my purpose in calling."

Sandy reached across her desk and grabbed the next file from the stack as she said, "Yes, let's. I have a ton of cases to get through in preparation for tomorrow." She began to scribble something on a page labeled "Notes."

"Fine. I was calling to see if perhaps we could reach some kind of a plea deal for my Gurganus fellow."

Sandy stopped writing and looked at the ceiling thoughtfully. "Sure. I'll dismiss the sexual assault, he enters a plea of guilty on the carnal knowledge and the rape." Sandy picked up her pen again and began finishing making her note on the inside cover of the file. Then she closed the file and set it to aside so she could get to the next one. She realized that Samuel had not responded.

She held still, carefully listening into the receiver. Hearing nothing, she said, "Mr. Samuel? Did I lose you?"

There was another pause before he said in an eerily calm voice, "I'm here. I was just waiting patiently for the real plea offer, as surely that could not have been it."

Sandy rolled her eyes and made no attempt to hide the disgust in her voice.

"Listen," she said. "What did you think I would offer? We have his DNA, we have the child's identification, we have his fingerprints. Hell, he practically left his business card taped to the child's head!"

Sandy stopped speaking and listened for his response. She heard nothing but another long pause. Finally, she said calmly, "Listen, Samuel, I know you are just doing your job, okay. But I'm doing mine, too. Off the record, this is one case where I don't mind putting away the defendant forever."

"Sandy," Samuel began, "what happens if there is no DNA? What happens when you can't find it? After all, tomorrow is your last day, and I've not got the call from you, with your voice gushing in excitement, telling me that you found the only real evidence that would connect him to the crime."

Sandy responded quickly, even though truthfully she feared that he was correct. "So, if you are so confident, then why call me today?

Call tomorrow and boast about helping a rapist run loose to rape another baby!"

Samuel audibly sighed. Sandy could feel that he was going to say something, but it was either something he didn't want to say or else he was carefully choosing his words.

Finally, he said, "I suppose I deserve that in some small way, but let me ask you, as you clearly sit high above us all on some moral mountain that I am apparently incapable of climbing. Have you ever done the wrong thing in a case? Now, I don't mean wrong in the eyes of the law—but maybe you offered a plea to someone when the evidence was stronger. You know, doing the wrong thing for the right reason. Like, perhaps, for someone who deserved a second chance or someone your gut told you was innocent even though the evidence said you could convict them?"

Sandy's memory immediately flashed to a young man named Louis Jr., or LJ for short. Sandy was a brand new assistant district attorney sitting next to a senior attorney in the juvenile division when L.J. came to her just before court went into session. He was fourteen years old and had broken into a newly constructed home that was not yet occupied. He was average height for his age, rather thin, and appeared to be wearing clothes that he may have slept in. His hair was a little long and, although it was brushed, appeared somehow out of sorts. She watched in fascination as he approached her. He didn't make eye contact, hesitated several times, and appeared to Sandy to have a gentle nature.

The senior attorney, Charley, was busy working out the morning's plea bargains with the defense attorneys while Sandy called out the names of defendants who had no attorneys, to get their side of the story.

L.J. approached her with his dad. "I'm Louis, and this here is my boy, L.J." Louis, the young man's dad, was also of average height and build, but his callused, oil-stained hands told her that he was a hard worker. His pulled-back ponytail and the nervous way in which he wrung his ball cap—the logo of which matched the logo on his shirt—made it clear to her that he was out of his element in a courtroom.

Sandy introduced herself.

"Now, Miss, my boy here, he ain't always bright. He ain't done the right thing at that next-door house. I ain't the sort to tolerate his foolishness. I want you to know he was punished, and I mean punished good." Sandy glanced at L.J., who was slightly redder now than when he had initially approached her.

"See, since his momma done up and left us, we been doin' the best we can. He done acted a fool, but he ain't a bad kid. He done something stupid, but he ain't bad. I suppose I could do better at trainin' him in the ways men should act. Anyhow, can we just pay a fine and go? I cain't miss no more work. We're barely gettin' by, anyway."

Sandy believed every word, although she couldn't say why. She argued with Charley for ten minutes before they finally agreed to let L.J. pay restitution for the damage he caused to the door when he broke into the house. Charley bet that L.J. would be back in trouble within six months. Charley was wrong. Still, Sandy knew she did the right thing in not prosecuting that kid, although she clearly had the evidence to convict him.

Even with the memory of L.J., Sandy knowingly lied to Samuel when she responded. "No, Samuel. I do my best to follow the black letter of the law, even when it's not popular. But this isn't about me, is it? This is about your client, the rapist. How dare you suggest to me that I 'do the wrong thing for the right reason' when the one thing I know I have right in this case is that *your* client is a rapist."

Samuel sighed again. "Wow, you just don't get it, do you?" Samuel paused. Sandy visualized him sitting at an oversized and expensive desk thinking of his response.

"Sandy, please tuck your anger into your purse, as you won't be needing it for the next several minutes. Let's you and I think about how this plays out. First option, you find the evidence and convict my client to the fullest and spend the night with all your little friends celebrating your great lawyering. Ah, but wait, there is another possibility. Let's dare to suggest that you don't find the DNA evidence. You go to trial on the hopes that a traumatized child remembers the details of a very brutal attack and the man who did it. Maybe you win. But, and it's a very big but, maybe you lose.

"Here is my suggestion. There is a very small window here for you and I. Tomorrow we know whether you have it or not. But today, we can negotiate with those possibilities hanging over both our heads. So, for example, I could suggest to my client that it may be safer to take a plea bargain, admit to child abuse, and serve five years rather than risk a life sentence. Do you understand, Sandy? Are you reading between the lines?"

Sandy was taken aback. Could there be a part, albeit a small part, of Samuel that was human? Basically, he was suggesting that he help her put his client away for five years rather than risk none. They both knew the odds were growing ever greater that she would lose her evidence—and he didn't want to risk his client's walking free, either. She said in a barely audible whisper, "You know he did it. You want him to go to prison."

Samuel didn't respond. They sat quietly on the phone for a moment. He finally said, "You know, Sandy, a bird in the hand is worth more than two in the bush. No, seriously, it really is. I've looked at the same evidence that you have. I know what it says. Yes, I will argue that the lab was wrong or that the child doesn't remember correctly—and a dozen other things. Or you and I can work this out. We can make the right thing happen. But remember, it all changes tomorrow when you miss the deadline. I can't tell my client to take a deal when I know that you can't prove your case."

"What do you suggest? I gave you my offer. I'll dismiss the child abuse if he pleads guilty to carnal knowledge of a juvenile and rape."

"I can't recommend that. Under that scenario, he spends the rest of his life in prison."

"As he should," Sandy exclaimed.

"But why would he take a plea to the maximum? If he is going to get the maximum, he might as well roll the dice and go to trial. Hell, he couldn't get worse! No, I suggest he pleads guilty to the child abuse and that you dismiss the carnal knowledge and the rape."

"No deal!" Sandy was incensed. "Samuel, he'll get five years minus time already served. He'll be in prison for less than three years."

"Fine. Listen. I will suggest to him that he pleads guilty to the carnal knowledge. Dismiss the rape and the child abuse. He'll get ten years. He has to serve at least eight."

Sandy's head was spinning. Was this a trick? Eight years? She suddenly had a vision of Dori and her parents. How would she tell them that he will be out in eight years?

"Samuel. Listen. I just can't do it. It's not enough time. He will be back out there again, free to rape another child. Please. I need the rape charge."

Samuel sounded equally disappointed when he said, "I get it. You can't give him less time for the same reason that I can't suggest he plead to more. At the end of the day, we are lawyers. It is incumbent upon us to do the best we can for our clients. In this case, Counselor, we will just have to respectfully disagree."

Sandy leaned back in her chair. She was disheartened. "I suppose you are right."

"Well, good luck tomorrow," he said.

"Thanks. Thanks." She hung up. While she questioned her decision and knew that she was risking winning her case because the DNA evidence was missing, she couldn't bear to agree to give Gurganus less than he deserved.

It was early afternoon the next day when she got the call. It was Friday, D-day for the evidence. She had expected his call any minute.

"Thank you for holding; this is Sandy." She answered the call cheerfully and hopefully.

"Well, you don't owe me dinner, but maybe you will go with me anyway," said the equally cheerful voice of Detective Curtis.

"What?" said Sandy, having heard but hoping she had misunderstood. Without a conscious effort, she shook her head no. There was a long pause before he finally answered her.

"I couldn't find it, honey," he sighed. "I know you are disappointed."

"Disappointed," she said slowly. "I'm shocked. Today's my deadline. I lose my DNA evidence." She paused before continuing in a dry, even voice. "I'm so screwed."

Sandy hung up the phone without waiting for a response. The weight of the news had made her forget that there was even someone on the other end. She turned her chair to stare blankly out the window. She felt no emotions. Just emptiness.

Outside her window and down on the street, the world bustled busily. A child stood staring at the ground, eyes fixed on the ice cream he had just dropped, while his mother tugged on his hand to pull him away. A well-suited man pushed past them while having a serious conversation on his cell phone. The bus stopped to pick up half a dozen people who had been waiting at a shaded bus stop.

No one knew that minutes ago, Sandy's world was shaken.

How long she sat there feeling the weight of this blow is anyone's guess. At some point, though, Sandy picked up her purse and left the office early for the first time in her career. She didn't worry about Monday. She didn't worry about preparing. She only worried about getting to the cabin.

She sat patiently through the afternoon traffic. She drove quickly along the interstate and through the wooded country roads until her car found itself safe at the cabin.

Sandy parked her car next to Old Gray's empty spot, grabbed her purse, and calmly walked to the door. Once inside, she mindlessly put water in the microwave to boil for hot tea, and then she went to her room to change into something more comfortable. She imagined that she would sit on the front porch swing and drink hot tea while watching the sun fade.

Realizing that she hadn't brought a change of clothes, she went into her parents' room and grabbed her dad's jogging pants and an old T-shirt. She slipped off her shoes and threw her skirt on the bed. She could feel the cool wood floor under her feet as she jumped inside her father's worn jogging pants. Spotting her dad's old slippers, she tucked her feet warmly inside them before throwing her jacket and then her undershirt onto the bed. Sandy quickly unfolded and began putting on her father's T-shirt.

She stopped, frozen.

Her father's T-shirt.

She could see herself in the full-length mirror that was attached to the cleanly painted white door of the closet. She imagined him standing there in that same shirt, one that bore the words "Crescent City Classic" along with a drawing of the downtown New Orleans area.

With that image in mind of her father wearing that shirt, Sandy began to cry. The emotions she had so carefully held back that day came pouring out uncontrollably. She was mad. She was furiously mad.

Like a child, Sandy threw herself onto the bed and screamed into the forgiving pillows. Her hair stuck her face that was moist with sweat and streaming tears. She had no words, just deep, sorrowful screams—until her voice gave way and she grew tired.

Sandy fell asleep crying. She never left her father's bed.

Sandy awoke late the next morning, shocked that she had slept past ten, as if she were a teenager. She piddled around the cabin, where she found herself pouting, crying hysterically, and sleeping for hours on end. She was too tired and frustrated to watch television, read a book, or enjoy the porch swing.

She lost track of the hours. Days, even. Until Monday late morning, when she, still wearing his clothes, was awakened by her father.

"My goodness, honey," he exclaimed as he walked into the room to find her sprawled across his bed. "It's nearly eleven. Are you really still sleeping?"

Her father sat on the bed next to her and felt her forehead, as if he believed that she must be sick to be behaving this way.

Not feeling a fever, he began looking around the room. Empty and dirty glasses, bowls, an ice cream container, and a chocolate syrup bottle were scattered all over his usually tidy bedroom. *Something is definitely out of order,* he thought to himself.

"What day is it?" Sandy asked sleepily, as if she really could not care less what day it was but was trying to make small talk.

Her father studied her face. He watched her stretch and then close her eyes again, as if dozing back off.

"Honey," he said, shaking her shoulder, "it's Monday. You missed work today."

"Really?" she said, with only the slightest hint of concern in her voice.

From the other room, she heard, "Mr. Morgan. Mr. Morgan, is everything all right?"

Sandy sat upright in the bed. Her dad responded over his shoulder, "Yes, son, she's in here."

Sandy shook her head and began to protest, but before she had gotten out any words, she beheld a familiar shape in the doorway.

"You've had me worried sick," Bradley Curtis said, leaning comfortably against the door and looking relieved.

Her father turned back to her, the smile on his face quickly fading when he saw the shock on hers.

"I've … I've … been … busy, that's all," she said, smoothing her hair and catching a glimpse of her unwashed face and hair in the mirror. "Exactly what are you doing here, anyway?" she demanded angrily.

"Your dad helped me find you," Curtis responded cheerily.

"That reminds me, dear," her father began quickly, patting her hand, "I am quite late for my tee time. I will catch up with you later." Then he stood, planted a kiss on her forehead, and turned to leave. "By the way, dear, perhaps a shower would wake you up a bit. Just a suggestion." He shrugged his shoulders, and then he turned and left.

Sandy crossed her arms on her chest and huffed. She leaned against the headboard and stared straight ahead.

"You are adorable in the morning," Curtis said, still smiling.

Sandy rolled her eyes as she grabbed a pillow and hid her face in it.

"You know what?" he said, but then he answered himself without waiting for a response from her. "I am hungry. I bet you are, too. I'm going to get us lunch, then I'm coming back here, and you and I are going to sit on that porch and relax. What do you think?"

Sandy peeked from under the pillow at him. He was still leaning casually against the doorjamb, his legs crossed at the ankles. She didn't want to look, didn't want to take inventory of his handsome, crooked smile. *Damn*, she cursed herself.

"I'll take that as a yes, Sleeping Beauty. You have about half an hour to manage without me, and then you have my undivided attention for the rest of the afternoon." He smiled that smile at her as she feigned aggravation. He shook his head and turned to leave.

As soon as she heard the door click, she made a mad dash for the shower. She scrambled for a razor, then shampoo. *Damn soap*, she thought as she fought to get the last of it out of the bottle.

Dry off. Oh no, clothes. I have no clothes. Back into Dad's closet. Mom's shorts! Baggy, but they'll do. Perfume. Great—Mom's cheap stuff. Mom's leftover makeup—not my color. No choice. Why am I nervous? Hair dryer. Where is that hair dryer? Here we go.

Sandy walked out of the bathroom thirty minutes later and felt like a new person. She nervously stepped into the open living room.

"Bradley," she called softly. There was no response. She went to the back door and felt the butterflies when she saw his truck. She nearly ran to the opposite end of the house and opened the screen door again, calling out to him: "Bradley."

"Over here," came his familiar, deep voice.

Sandy came down the steps to find that he had spread the comforter from her bed out onto the grass and had a bucket of chicken, along with plates, forks, and coleslaw. "Why, you are a regular picnic prince, now, aren't you?"

"Anything for you," he responded sarcastically, despite the fact that what he just said was true.

Sandy took her place on the comforter. Curtis lay on his side next to her before leaning over and fixing her a plate.

"So, how in the world did you find this, the most beautiful place on Earth?"

That was how it started. Right there on that blanket. The two talked for several hours without taking a break. It was just what Sandy needed at that exact moment. To smile, to joke—to forget. Even if it was short-lived.

After their nearly four-hour picnic, the two packed up the leftovers, plates, and comforter. They headed back inside to freshen up their tea glasses, and then they returned outdoors and took comfortable seats on the porch swing.

They may have sat there forever, except for the fact that the darkness that had stolen Sandy's heart was about to make a play for Curtis's, as well.

"So, I take it you are not still mad at me?" he asked.

"Mad at you?" Sandy responded.

"You know, the missing evidence."

Without warning, Sandy snapped back into her anger. She could picture Gurganus's hands, his short, thick fingers, callused and rough, tugging at her. She could smell the smoke on his breath.

Sandy couldn't speak. She knew that if she said a word, she would not be able to control her emotions. She struggled to hide her tears.

Minutes passed before she realized that Bradley was staring at her. She glanced at him, unable to look him in the eye.

He watched her in silence, until finally he said in a soft voice, "You know, I remember what you were wearing the first time I ever saw you."

Her eyebrows arched questioningly.

"You were coming up the stairs of the courthouse. Out front. You had on a black pantsuit. You know, the one with the short, calf-length pants."

"Capris?"

"Yeah, I guess. Anyway, you were coming up the stairs and were near the top when I came out that front door. You had on a green and black striped shirt beneath your jacket. Little black shoes. So serious—and beautiful."

Several moments passed before Sandy asked, "Why are you telling me this?"

"It's simple. That moment. That one moment changed my life. I wanted to climb right inside that briefcase and go with you wherever you went. It was more than love at first sight. I wanted to know you. You made me curious. You made me interested.

"I did everything I could think of to get to handle petty crimes on the off chance that I could work with you. I couldn't find out enough about you. The first time you accepted an invitation to spend more than just a few seconds with me, I didn't want to screw it up. You were too important to me. Literally, since the moment I first saw you."

Sandy sat back on the swing, drinking in his tender words. "Wow," she said, "I never knew."

Curtis leaned back, too. His arm lay across the back of the swing. His hand brushed the loose strands of hair from her face. "Of course not," he said, shrugging. "That's a little much to tell someone on a first date, don't you think?" They both smiled.

Curtis sat up and turned to face her, leaning back so he could get a good look at her as he said, "I want you to trust me. I need you to trust me. Whatever is going on here, I can handle it. You can trust me with it."

Sandy paused. "I don't know what you mean."

"I think you do."

"No," she said angrily, "I don't!"

Curtis snapped his finger and pointed at her. "Right there. Right there it is. See how angry you became. C'mon. I've done dozens of these cases with you. How many times have we laughed, saying, 'If we don't get them this time, chances are they'll be in here again next week'? I know you are angry that we didn't get him this time, but there is more to it for you, I can just tell."

Sandy stood up angrily. "Look, it's just different, okay?"

"Why?"

"Why," she said while standing, her tone exaggerated. "Why? Because it is. I want this bastard to pay," she practically yelled at him.

"I don't understand," he said.

"What's to understand?" she shrieked. "I can't stand to see that disgusting smile. His nasty face twisting into a hateful grin while he walks free." Sandy's voice was getting louder. She was growing more frantic.

"Sandy," Curtis said as he stood to reach out to her.

"No," she said, her shriek deepening as she glared at him, "you don't understand. I *have* to do it. It's my job. Dori is counting on me." As Curtis moved closer to console her, she yelled, "Don't come near me. *You* don't get it! He'll rape again. That sick bastard. He'll rape again!"

Curtis grabbed her arm; his dark eyebrows were arched in utter confusion. "Honey, calm down."

"Let go of me!" she screamed uncontrollably, viciously yanking her body to free herself from his clutch.

Curtis pulled her close to him, trying to comfort her, saying things like, "I don't understand"; "Breathe, honey"; and "Stay calm."

Sandy was hysterical. She sharply pulled herself from his grip and made an attempt to climb the stairs that led off the porch. In her rush, she lost her footing and fell, crying out, down all three stairs.

Curtis rushed to her as she lay in a heap at the bottom of the stairs. She was crying so deeply that he couldn't decipher her words.

"Are you okay? Look at me, are you okay? I don't understand. Are you hurt? Please, Sandy, I just don't understand."

Sandy lifted her head and said through her sobs, nearly screaming, *"He raped me. He raped me.* Don't you get it? He raped *me!"* Sandy lay her head in the soft afternoon grass and sobbed.

Curtis loosened his grip on her arm and slipped her small hand into his. "Honey, you were raped by someone?"

"No. Not someone. I was raped by *him.* I was raped by that sick bastard. I was a baby. I was just a baby. Third grade. He pulled me behind the shed, his hands groping me," she cried, her legs kicking at the grass as if she were still in that moment, fighting her assailant. "I didn't know what to do. I wasn't sure what he was doing. By the time I realized he was hurting me, it was too late." Sandy flung her head back onto the soft grass, whimpering. "I was just a baby!"

Curtis sat there patiently listening, dumbfounded. He fell to the ground next to her limp body, not exactly sure what to say. "What ... how did ... did your dad know?"

Sandy cried through her answer. "Sure. Are you kidding me! Everyone knew. My teachers, my friends—even the lady at the grocery store asked me about it. It was humiliating. They arrested him. He went to trial. I had to testify. I was just a little kid! I had to sit across from the bastard and say out loud what he did to me."

Sandy paused as if thinking. She was sad and quiet, recalling the trial. "But I couldn't do it. I just sat there. I was petrified." Sandy stared ahead, her mind miles away as she continued. "They wanted me to identify him. Point him out. Tell about the cuts on my private parts—which I didn't even know the names for. I had to look at pictures of myself and say out loud, 'Yes. Yes, that is me,' while he watched!"

She had a brief but distinct memory of his face looking at her while she testified. Sandy stood up. She didn't know where she was going, but she had to get away from this conversation. As she stood, she winced in pain. She had apparently fallen on her knee harder than she thought.

She could feel him lift her up. She held onto his neck and allowed him to carry her. Her eyes were tightly closed, tears streaming from them, as Curtis whispered, "There, there, I have you. I have you, honey, I have you. Sh, try not to cry."

Moments later, she felt him bend and also felt the soft bed under her. She opened her eyes to find him walking out the door. Her heart sank. *He knows my secret. I've lost him. He's probably calling for backup. I'm going to lose my job. I'm going to lose my license.* She rolled over to bury her face in the pillow to hide her shameful tears.

To her surprise, she felt cold ice on her knee a few minutes later. She pulled herself to a sitting position. She wiped her tears and looked at him earnestly.

"I thought you left," she whimpered.

He smiled a faint but soft smile. "Hardly, my love. I'm here. I'm staying right here next to you. For as long as you let me."

"Do you hate me?" she said quietly, afraid to make eye contact.

His arched eyebrows gave away his question: "Why would I?"

She continued. "You know as well as I do that it's illegal. I can't prosecute this case. Now that you know, you have a duty to report …" Her voice broke.

"Sh, now," he said, brushing back the loose strands of hair from her face. As she calmed down, he couldn't help but ask her, "What happened? At the trial, I mean, when you couldn't testify?"

Sandy's face lost all expression. She stared straight ahead and said blankly, "Dismissal. Dismissal because of insufficient evidence." Then, looking at him, she continued. "It is my fault, you know. It was my fault then because I sat there like an idiot saying, 'I don't know, I don't know'—and then he walked."

"Oh, now. Stop that. You were just a little kid." Bradley comforted her.

Sandy looked at her hands as she wrung them in her lap. "It is my fault now. It is my fault that he went free and did this to Dori and to who knows how many others. If I don't bury him this time, I will wear the blood of every new victim he takes." Sandy began crying softly through her words. "So, see, I feel like I had no choice but to take this case. If you feel you must report me, then go for it. We all have to own our decisions. I knew the risk of getting caught when I did this. I took the risk. I'll own the consequences, if any."

"Now, now," Curtis said quietly. As if thinking out loud, he added, "I wonder why he hasn't said anything. About you, I mean. I wonder why he hasn't tried to get you removed."

"Oh. It's simple. He doesn't remember me," she said weakly.

Curtis couldn't hide the fact that he was shocked. He sat up straight on the bed to better look at her. "He doesn't remember you?" He stared at her blankly for a moment, digesting her words. His expression changed from shocked to confused, and then to angry. "He doesn't even remember you?" He harshly demanded an answer. He stood and walked to the window and stared out of it, still enraged.

He turned back to her and asked quietly, "I bet you think of him every day, don't you?"

Sandy shook her head yes, embarrassed to admit that it was true. She cleared her throat to remove the lump before continuing. "It's the smell of smoke that I remember most. That and the way his hands looked. They were thick and callused, and they pulled on me … I still have vivid memories."

"That son of a bitch," Curtis said under his breath, trying to prevent himself from punching the wall. "How can he not even remember you?" He started shaking his head. "Look, Sandy, I don't know what the fuck to do. I'm going to kill that bastard. Do you know how many years his nasty ass has been doing this to kids? How many kids has he put his hands on? This is ridiculous." He started pacing in front of the window, running his fingers nervously through his hair. Several seconds passed before his pace slowed.

"I just ... I need a minute," he said as he began to cross the room to leave. When he reached the door, he turned and said to her over his shoulder, "I am right outside. I have to sort this out in my head. I need to think it through, but I am staying right here. You know, in case you need me."

As he walked out of the room, she whispered sadly, "I do, you know. I do need you."

Sandy called in sick on Tuesday.

In fact, they both did.

CHAPTER 12

"You must be Dori!" Sandy said in her best child-friendly voice as she approached the little girl in the lobby of the district attorney's office.

Dori, a beautiful little girl with petite features, was lying on her belly and coloring in her princess coloring book. She began to stand.

"Yes, ma'am," she said softly as she pulled down on her dress, nervously trying to rid it of invisible wrinkles.

"My name is Ms. Sandy."

Sandy stretched out her hand to shake the child's while she bent over and said cheerfully, "And did you bring your parents?" as if she didn't see them sitting right behind her.

Dori, feeling very grown up, smiled nervously and said, "I did. That's them," as she pointed to her parents.

Dori's mother was a thin, beautiful woman who resembled her child. She wore a sharp tan pantsuit and heels. She pushed her sunglasses to the top of her head, where they held back long blonde tresses. Now seeing her deep blue eyes, Sandy could tell that they bore a redness that only hours of crying could produce. Dori's father could hardly muster a smile as he reached out his hand to shake Sandy's. Even though he wore casual jeans and a blazer, she could tell that he was all business. He appeared so nervous that she thought he might actually vomit.

"Mr. and Mrs. Dauzat," Sandy said, shaking their hands and smiling at them apologetically, "let's step into my office so we have some privacy."

Sandy's office was near the end of the hall. Her paralegal, whom she shared with two other assistant district attorneys, often teased her and said that she had the almost-corner office. Still, Sandy loved the office. Although it was a small space, when she walked in the door, she was opposite large picture windows that spanned the room's length.

Sandy's small, cluttered desk faced the door; a credenza spanned most of the length of the windows. The credenza bore the burden of various stacks of papers and files. Positioned neatly against the wall behind her desk were several blown-up exhibits from her more challenging cases. Sandy enjoyed flipping through them occasionally to reflect.

With the exception of a small toy box near the door, the rest of the room was filled with bookshelves upon which sat neatly organized books. That is, with the exception of the shelf nearest her desk, on which there were several books sitting half on, half off, on their sides, with tabs sticking out and pages bent. In explaining to her dad why these appeared this way, she said, "Hey, those are the ones I really use."

As the Dauzats reached Sandy's office and settled into their chairs, Sandy pointed to the large box near the door. "Dori, see that box? It is a treasure box. I thought maybe you would like to look in there and pick out a treasure. Would you like that?"

"Yes, ma'am," she said quietly. The girl walked slowly to the box and lifted the lid.

"Do you have many children that have to come here?" Mr. Dauzat said, watching his daughter and intentionally not looking at Sandy. His voice cracked a little when he said the word *many*.

Sandy sighed as she watched Dori slowly and carefully begin to look inside the box. "Unfortunately, yes. One is too many, of course, but I have several dozen a year." Sandy turned back to the Dauzats. "I have never had an easy one, that I can tell you. I want you to know that I have Dori's best interests at heart. I will treat her like my own. Today, I will explain to her what will happen in court. I will then ask that she tell me the story of what happened to her that night. I will need the two of you to be strong, you know, for her sake. The courtroom is very scary. Gurganus will be there, and it will be very intimidating for her. Your tears and fear will reflect on her, so, as hard as it is, please try to control your emotions until the end."

Dori walked up to her mother holding a "treasure." "Wow," Mrs. Dauzat said, "a pink horse and pink brush for her mane. Now, what do you say?"

Dori smiled at Sandy. "Thank you," she said. Then she asked her mother, "Can you open it?"

"Yes," she said, "but not until after we talk with Ms. Sandy."

"'Kay," said the child as her mother pulled her onto her lap.

"Dori, did your mom and dad explain to you who I am and why we are visiting with each other today?"

Dori nodded yes.

"I want to tell you a little bit about my job and then tell you how you can help me do my job, okay?"

Dori nodded yes again.

"I am a lawyer. There are a bunch of different types of lawyers, and they work for a bunch of different types of people. I am a special kind of lawyer. I work for our state, and I try to help protect people in our state from people who do crimes. Do you know what a crime is?"

Dori began, "Um, well, it's like when you break a toy and it wasn't yours, or you borrow a toy and you didn't ask if you could."

"Well, yes, kind of like that. Sometimes we do things that hurt people accidentally, and sometimes people hurt other people on purpose. My job is to stop grown-ups who hurt children on purpose. The way I do that is by learning who these grown-ups are and telling the judge about them. But it can't just be me who says it. I need anyone who knows about it to tell the judge, too, so that he knows that what I am saying is true and so that he understands exactly what happened to the child. Then he decides if and how to punish the grown-up. Do you understand?"

Dori nodded yes.

"I'm going to ask you lots of questions today. Then, in a couple of weeks, I'm going to ask you the same questions again, but this time we will be in a courtroom and in front of the judge. Have you ever been to a courtroom before?"

Dori shook her head no, but she said, "I think I saw one on TV. Before, though."

"Well, great!" Sandy said in an upbeat tone of voice. "It is probably almost just like that! We will be sure to go and see the courtroom either before or after we talk to the judge, okay, Mom?" Sandy said, looking at Mrs. Dauzat.

Mrs. Dauzat smiled and nodded, saying, "Yes, just like on TV."

Sandy continued. "I just want you to tell the truth, okay? I want you always to remember that you didn't do anything wrong. You are not in trouble, and you don't need to be scared. You know, even grown-ups get nervous in court. Remember, even though you might get nervous, we are all there with you, okay?"

Dori nodded yes.

"Okay, now let's talk about you. Dori, honey, have you ever had a grown-up hurt you?"

Dori slowly nodded yes.

"Have you told your mom and dad about this?"

Dori didn't make eye contact as she nodded yes.

"All right, honey. Moving your head yes and no is okay with us, because we understand you. When you talk in front of the judge, though, you will have to answer with words. Okay? Because there will be a lady sitting near you who will be typing everything that everyone says so that later everyone can remember. So, why don't we practice now, all right?"

Dori said quietly, "'Kay."

"Great. Now, where were you when you got hurt?"

"I was at Uncle Lee's house."

"Did you know the grown-up that hurt you?"

Dori shook her head no.

"Did Uncle Lee hurt you?"

Dori raised her eyebrows and said, "No," emphatically.

"Okay. Where were you the first time you saw the man that hurt you?"

"Down by, like, where the stove is."

"Now, Uncle Lee said he thought you were sleeping. Did you fall asleep and wake up?"

"I, well, I did, but Daddy said he was going to get me early cuz we had tickets to a party at the zoo and we was going to go. So, when I waked up, I didn't know if it was early yet. Uncle Lee was sleeping, too, so I tried to be quiet and look at his clock." Dori shrugged her shoulders before continuing. "But his clock points at what time it is, it doesn't write it. On the stove, it writes the time. So I went down all the stairs to see the time on the stove."

"Ah, I see," Sandy said. "And do you remember what time it was?"

"Um," Dori pondered. "No, I forgot it already," Dori said, shaking her head no, which caused her long blonde strands to wave.

"That's okay. That's a perfect answer. When you don't remember, just say you don't. What happened after you looked at the time?" Sandy was sitting on the side of her desk, leaning in as closely as she could without falling off the chair.

"Well, I saw the scary guy."

"I see. What was he doing?" Sandy asked.

"He was standing by the back door and he was waving at me." Dori shook her hands feverishly back and forth, as the defendant must have done. "He was saying words, but I didn't hear them good enough. So I got by the door, but I still couldn't hear." Dori paused, apparently regretting the choice she had made that night.

"So I opened the door." Dori began looking at her hands, growing uncomfortable. She quickly looked at her mother and then again at her hands.

"It's okay," Mrs. Dauzat whispered in her ear as she pulled her closer.

"What happened when you opened the door?" Sandy asked softly.

"I don't, see, I'm not sure, but I fell down on the grass."

"Did the man grab you or push you?"

"I'm not ... I don't know," Dori said anxiously, shaking her head from side to side.

"All right, it's okay. Whenever you don't remember, I want you to just say that you don't know. It's okay not to remember. Okay, so what happened after you landed on the grass?"

"Well, um, I ..." Dori searched for words.

Mr. Dauzat abruptly stood up. "You know, I, uh, I think I will go find us something to drink."

Sandy looked at the child's father, having almost forgotten that he was there. He didn't make eye contact, but he couldn't hide the fact that his eyes were brimming with tears. He left before anyone could respond to him. As he closed the door, Mrs. Dauzat said in a whisper, "This is so hard for him." Sandy nodded yes understandingly before turning her attention back to Dori.

"All right, honey, we were talking about after you landed on the grass," Sandy prodded, wanting this to be over as much as the family did.

"I tried to get up. He just, like, grabbed at my feet cuz I was trying to crawl away. He pulled me to where I was sorta under him, and his hand was, like, this big." With her little hands, she indicated a size of about two feet wide. "And he had it over my head by my mouth. I was trying to call Uncle Lee, and he was saying stuff in my ear, and he smelled like a fireplace."

"Do you remember what he said?" Sandy asked softly, she herself remembering the smell of smoke on Gurganus's breath.

"He said stuff like, 'Hold still,' 'Don't wiggle,' and, 'Sh.'"

"What happened next?"

"My legs got cold and I knew something was happening down there by my bottom," Dori said, pointing at her upper thigh and buttocks area, in case Sandy didn't know where that was.

"Okay. What do you mean by cold?"

"Well, like, my nightie came up by my middle, and he was yanking on my undies."

"All right, honey, you are doing great," Sandy said, managing a weak smile. "What did he do next?"

"Well … I could feel him poke my privates … and I got scared cuz it hurt. So I bit on his finger and got to move away." Dori, who had been staring at her hands, looked up. "But when I got by the porch, he got my leg again."

"Did he lie on top of you again, honey?" Sandy asked, trying to focus on her own breathing so as not to break down and cry.

"No. He was really, really mad and yelled at me, 'You wanna wiggle?'" Dori wrinkled her nose and used the ugliest tone of voice she could muster to imitate the man. "And then he said that again, like, five times—and then an angel took my mind away."

Sandy's eyebrows rose. "An angel took your mind away?" she asked, confused.

"I told her that." Mrs. Dauzat interrupted and grabbed a tissue from Sandy's desk to dab her eyes. "I'm sorry. She doesn't remember after that moment. I think that's when he hit her on the side of her head, so I told her an angel took her mind away so that she wouldn't have to be there while he hurt her. I didn't know how to explain it. I mean, she woke up in such pain; I had to explain it somehow. I didn't want to lie but …" Mrs. Dauzat began to unravel quickly and lose control of her emotions. "I didn't know how to tell her. I mean, he ripped her from one side to the other …"

"No, no, it's okay. Really, it's okay," Sandy said softly, moving to the chair next to Mrs. Dauzat that now sat vacant since Mr. Dauzat had left. Sandy put her hand on Mrs. Dauzat's arm. "I think it's a lovely explanation."

Mrs. Dauzat took several deep breaths and managed to regain some of her composure. "Seven weeks," she said shakily. "Seven weeks she lay in that hospital bed. She was voiceless. Nearly two months. I thought she had brain damage or was a mute or worse. I didn't know how awful it was, what she remembered, if she was having nightmares. I was so relieved"—her voice began cracking—"I was so relieved that she didn't remember the worst of it."

"I completely understand," Sandy said as she beheld Dori's sad expression as she watched her mother cry. *All of this rehashing is just as bad as the crime,* Sandy thought.

Mrs. Dauzat continued. "She'll carry the scars for the rest of her life. She'll never have a child of her own …" Mrs. Dauzat was crying now, holding her head in her hands.

"I'm sorry. I wish I knew what to say," Sandy said, helpless.

Dori gently placed her hand on her mother's arm. "Mommy, don't cry." Then, in a new tone of voice, as if she were the parent, she said, "You know, Paw-Paw always says that everything happens for a reason. Maybe now I can live with you forever and not have to go away and get married and have babies!" Dori said, almost pleased.

Mrs. Dauzat smiled at Dori's innocence. She wiped her tears and sat up straight, pulling the child closer to her when she did so. She kissed the back of Dori's head. It was such a sweet exchange that Sandy almost felt as if she were invading their privacy.

"Dori, honey," Sandy asked with a smile, "are you ready to go find your daddy?"

CHAPTER 13

GURGANUS IS STANDING ON THE CORNER. HE HAS JUST MADE SOME quick cash at the art studio where he sold yet another one of mother's pieces. He is looking right to left, down the street. He has nowhere to be, so he decides to choose the most interesting direction.

He puts the cigarette in his mouth and leans in to light it. Taking a long drag, he lifts up his head to exhale. That's when he sees them.

He watches them, recognizing the man. *Oh yes, that's the asshole whose grass I mowed.*

A car pulls up. Gurganus and the driver exchange money and a small amount of cocaine. But it's not enough. He'll need more of the drug come morning. The car pulls away.

Gurganus crosses the street to catch up with Lawson. *That asshole lived right here somewhere.* He follows them home.

Oh yes, that house. I remember now, he thinks to himself.

Gurganus walks away. They are safe. At least until several hours later, when he returns. The goal is to steal. He needs the money. *Or some expensive shit,* he thinks.

He tries the window. Locked. He can't remember the layout of the house. Damn. He wanders around to the back.

He walks up the back porch. The security light goes on. *Shit.* He holds his breath. He plasters himself against the brick wall.

Minutes go by. Nothing. No noise. He moves again for the back door. Locked. *Fuck!*

He looks around the backyard. *It'll have to wait until he leaves during the day. … Wait, is that a window?*

Gurganus moves to cross the deck to reach the window when the security light comes on again. He looks back at the door to see if anyone is coming.

What's that? Oh yes, look at her frightened little face.

He motions to her. *I'm not so bad, little girl. Open the door for the big, bad wolf.*

She stands frozen. He smiles at her. *See, I'm okay.*

She moves slowly to the door and carefully unlocks it.

Gurganus swings it open, grabbing her by the arm.

Sandy sits straight up in the bed, immediately reaching for the light. She is sweaty and in a hot panic. The light isn't enough. She jumps out of bed and starts swatting at herself as if bugs are crawling all over her. "Shit, shit, shit," she says aloud.

She goes to the bathroom and splashes her face with water, telling herself to get a grip. She dries her face and practically runs to the front door. She checks the lock on her door—and all of her windows. She peeks out the bedroom window, expecting to see something, someone.

Sandy grabs her phone and gets back into bed. Every light is on. She dials a number and puts the phone to her ear.

"It's me." Sandy tries not to cry.

She continues. "It happened again. No, I'm okay. I just needed to talk to someone." She pauses as Curtis speaks.

"No, it was different this time. This time he just happened to see them on the street and followed them. He was going to rob Lawson. It didn't make a lot of sense, I know."

She pauses again as he speaks.

"Maybe it's because in my mind it is unresolved. You know, I just don't know how he knew that Dori was there that night. What brought him there? I don't get it."

Sandy listens but rolls her eyes and then says, "I know, I know. I understand that every piece doesn't always make sense. I just wish I could make sense of this one so that maybe I could sleep without having dreams about him and waking up."

She listens again and then says softly, "Hey, thanks. Sorry to wake you up. But would you mind just staying on the phone with me? I mean, just until I get a little drowsy?"

CHAPTER 14

August 11, Morning

TODAY, THERE IS ONE ITEM ON THE DOCKET. JUST ONE. *STATE VERSUS Gurganus.* Sandy turned to take inventory of the relatively empty courtroom. The defendant's father sat in the first row just behind the defense's table. What appeared to be a member of the press sat in the back row, feverishly pounding on the keyboard of her laptop.

Directly behind Sandy sat Dori, her parents, and Lee Lawson. Dori's mother, Laurie Dauzat, looked at Sandy with hopeful eyes. *It's all up to me,* Sandy thought. "I won't let you down," she heard herself say. Mrs. Dauzat smiled meekly. Out of the corner of her eye, Sandy could see Detective Bradley Curtis poke his head inside at the back door of the courtroom. She smiled at him and nodded as he motioned that he was going to be waiting outside.

At the defense table sat the defendant's attorney, Robert Samuel, who was busy organizing his exhibits so they were lined up just so. *Hmph, OCD,* thought Sandy. The very sight of Robert Samuel disgusted her. Today, he was wearing a very expensive, tailored light gray suit, a pressed white shirt, and a light pink tie. His shiny black shoes practically whistled as he walked, tugging on his jacket sleeves to ensure his gold cuff links saw the light of day. His gray hair seemed to serve as an accessory. Sandy was certain it would double as a helmet, should he ever decide to ride a motorcycle to court.

"Focus," she said to herself.

The heavy doors in the back of the courtroom opened. A sheriff from the detention center stepped in. Recognizing the green uniform shirt and the clatter of extra sets of handcuffs that the sheriff always seemed to carry, Sandy turned quickly to the Dauzats. "He's entering. Why don't you wait in the hall?"

Laurie Dauzat grabbed Dori's hand in a rush to get her out. Harold Dauzat grabbed Lee Lawson's arm. "C'mon, man." Lee didn't move but kept his eyes hard and set on the area where Gurganus was expected to appear. "Lee. It's not worth it, dude. C'mon."

Lee defiantly sat there, unwilling to budge.

Mr. Dauzat pulled harder. "Not today, man. I can't do this. I'm on the edge already. Let this happen the right way."

Perhaps it was Dauzat's tone, or perhaps it was his words, but Lee's facial expression changed in an instant. He looked his friend Harold in the eye and nodded yes, relenting at last. He stood, his every move appearing labored and difficult.

Sandy turned her attention to the beast entering the room. Suddenly, he didn't seem so big. Suddenly, she felt confident that justice would be served and, better yet, served by her. She stared at him hatefully. Her bottom lip began to quiver in anger. She leaned against the table, arms crossed.

Gurganus shuffled to the defense table. Samuel interrupted the quiet of the courtroom with a loud, "Good morning, Bruce!" Samuel extended his hand as if at a social function. "I'm ready; are you?"

Gurganus insisted that he was, indeed, ready.

Within a couple of minutes, Judge Bryson entered the courtroom. Moments later, he directed Sandy to begin her opening statement: "Let's get this show on the road, shall we?"

Sandy paused for a minute. Scribbled across the top of the yellow legal pad that held the secrets of her opening argument were the words "Gurganus Opening." Sandy carefully picked up her notes and began walking toward the podium, glancing one last time at the defendant. Not caring in the least, the defendant sat comfortably picking at his fingernails. Sandy gritted her teeth and prepared for battle.

She began. "Positive. Positive fingerprint identification. Positive photo ID from our minor victim." Then, pausing for effect, she continued by slowly raising and pointing her finger at the defendant. "We are positive that this defendant brutally raped and abused our minor victim, Adorina Dauzat.

"Your Honor, today you will hear from a tiny voice. A voice so small and innocent that it will oftentimes be hardly audible. Yet today, it will seem to roar when she points at this defendant and says, 'This is the man who raped me; this is the man who took the virginity of a five-year-old; this is the man who brutally tore me apart so much so that I will never have children; this is the man who so brutally abused me that I lay in a hospital bed for nearly seven weeks, unable to speak. But I can speak today, and today I will be heard." Sandy hesitated a moment before continuing.

"Your Honor, you will hear from the reporting officer, Officer Seth Tyler, who will describe the scene just moments after his arrival.

"You will hear from a veteran of the police force, Detective Bradley Curtis, who is an officer so detailed in his work that he left no stone unturned in his effort to determine who hurt this little girl.

"You will hear from our expert fingerprint analyst, Doug Crosby. He will say that he has been declared an expert on several occasions by this court and that his analysis was concrete. The fingerprints found on the items in the home belong to one person—this defendant," she said, pointing to Gurganus.

"You will hear from Lee Lawson, the family friend who had the misfortune of babysitting little Dori on the worst night of her life. He will explain to you his angst and fear, the nightmares he continues to have when he closes his eyes. He will tell you about finding a broken and torn Dori on his back lawn. He will tell you about the one time, many years ago, that he hired the defendant to do yard work. He will say that the defendant never touched tape or any other item inside his home."

"Finally, you will hear from Laurie Dauzat, who will tell you what it feels like to receive a call in the middle of the night from someone saying that your daughter, your little girl, is gone—never to return as the same innocent child you saw when you last left her.

"You will listen to their voices. You will hear the evidence. You will see the results of the tests. And then *you* will be positive." Sandy raised her hand and moved closer to the defendant, pointing. "You will be positive that this is the rapist. Positive that this defendant belongs in prison for the rest of his natural life."

Sandy stood motionless, her hand still pointing at Gurganus. Sure that her well-planned opening had the full effect she had intended, she began to move back to the prosecution's table. As she turned her back, she could hear the defendant say behind her, "Hmph. Right, lady. Good luck proving that shit."

Whether or not the judge could hear the defendant's actual words, Sandy couldn't guess, but he did intervene. "All right, all right. No speaking out of turn. Mr. Samuel, you're up!"

Robert Samuel stood. Without approaching the podium, he said sternly, "Positive?" Then, shrugging his shoulders and adding more volume to his voice, he said again, "Positive?"

He shook his head and chuckled, pretending that he was trying to remain unheard as he walked from behind the table to the podium. "Well, Your Honor, I am positive, too. Positive that my client is innocent. But more importantly, for the purposes of this trial, I am positive that the State will not be able to meet its burden of proof.

"Innocent," he said. Then he paused, pointing to his client. "Innocent. Innocent until proven guilty. Now, the State is going to parade a few little witnesses in here. The little girl will tell you that the beast that did this to her looks similar to our poor Mr. Gurganus here. The officer's going to tell you that the incident did, in fact, happen. The analyst will tell you that Mr. Gurganus's fingerprints were on a roll of tape, as you would expect them to be since he had worked in the home of the babysitter, Lee Lawson. The babysitter and the child's mother will testify that the little girl was all torn up. Heck, they may even shed a few tears.

"What none of them will tell you, though, Your Honor, is *who* did this. Who? The magic question. If my client were guilty, I'd be the first to walk away, Your Honor." Samuel held up his hand in a "stop" gesture and turned his head away from his client as if it hurt to look at him. "No, Your Honor, I just couldn't do it." Then, turning back toward his client and walking behind the table, ultimately to stand behind the defendant, he continued. "But the fact is that he didn't do it. Some rapist roams the streets this moment all because Mr. Gurganus had the misfortune of leaving his fingerprints on a roll of tape a couple of years ago." Then, resting his hands on the defendant's shoulders, he said, "It's simple, Your Honor. He didn't do it. I'm positive."

The judge raised his eyebrow as if double checking that Samuel's pause was truly the end of his opening statement. "All righty, then. State, please call you first witness. Wait—is anyone hot in here? Someone … hey, Tom," the judge said, motioning to the bailiff to adjust the thermostat. Hearing the air conditioner click on, the judge shifted in his seat to get more comfortable. Then he said, "All right, let's go."

"Your Honor," Sandy began, "I know this may be a little unusual, but I would like to call the minor victim first so that she doesn't have to wait in the hall all day."

The judge stared at her blankly. "Are you asking my permission, Counselor?" he asked.

Sandy sighed. "No, I just wanted to give you a heads-up, I guess." For a second, it occurred to her intention may have been to buy herself time. "The State calls Adorina Dauzat," she said confidently.

The bailiff set down the sports page and pulled himself from his chair. He slowly walked to the back of the courtroom and said loudly, "Adorina Dauzat." Sandy watched as he motioned with his hand for the child to come to him. Then he moved to the side, holding the door open.

Dori walked into the courtroom, pausing at the entrance to look up at the tall bailiff. He pointed straight ahead, and Dori turned back toward the courtroom and kept walking forward, glancing back once to make sure her parents were there. As expected, they were right behind her. She walked alone, with her parents holding hands behind her. While they looked petrified, Dori looked curious—not a happy curious, but a worried curious. Sandy thought that the girl looked as if she was walking into a doctor's office, worried that she was there to get a shot.

Dori, with parents in tow, approached the bar together. Sandy watched every second in awe. She couldn't hear any other sounds. She saw Dori approaching her fate and suddenly had distinct memories of this exact event in her own life. Sandy recalled the stillness of the room as she clung to her father's hand. She could hear the soft steps of her mother shortly behind her. She remembered reaching the swinging gate that separated the audience from the courtroom participants. She stopped, her father bending down to kiss her. "Be brave," he had whispered in her ear.

Dori made this same stop just before the swinging gate. Her father leaned over to kiss her. He, too, whispered something in her ear, and Dori nodded yes to him. Her mother touched Dori's cheek softly and gave her a wink and a smile.

Dori turned and pushed the gate open. Sandy went to her and took her hand. "Let me help you," she said as she led Dori to the witness stand. Dori took the two steps up and climbed onto the big wooden chair. Her feet dangled as she squirmed to get comfortable. She used her hands to smooth the light pink material of the skirt of her dress.

"You ready?" Sandy whispered.

"Uh-huh," Dori said nervously.

Sandy nodded to the court reporter, indicating that she was ready.

"Miss, could you raise your right hand?" the court reporter asked Dori.

Dori's eyes darted to Sandy, who immediately lifted her right hand so that Dori would know which hand to raise. Dori looked relieved and raised her little right hand high in the air.

"Do you swear to tell the truth, the whole truth, and nothing but the truth?"

Dori looked at Sandy again. Sandy nodded her encouragement. "I promise not to lie," Dori said emphatically.

The court reporter looked at the judge, who nodded yes, as if to say, "Close enough." The court reporter took her seat.

Sandy walked to the podium and gave Dori some simple directions before beginning her line of questions.

"Dori, how old are you?"

"I'm five."

"Do you go to school?"

"Yes, I'm a kindergartner. I go to Cathedral Academy, like my daddy did."

"Oh, good. Okay, Dori, could you tell me who Lee Lawson is?"

"You mean Uncle Lee?" Dori said hesitantly.

"Yes, your uncle Lee."

"Well, he's my uncle. He is my godfather, too, but I think that … well, I'm not sure exactly, but I think that means I'm like his special person. Like, he is my special uncle."

"How long have you known Uncle Lee?"

"How long?" Dori's face indicated that she thought the question was an odd one. "I don't remember not knowing him."

"Okay. Do you ever spend the night at his house?"

Dori looked a little confused, "I … well, I used to. Before I got hurt. I got to go all the time."

"Before you got hurt, when you used to stay at Uncle Lee's house, what are some of the things you used to do when you were there?"

"Well, Uncle Lee doesn't have any kids at his house. He doesn't even have a wife! So, when I go to his house, he calls it Dori Time, and he doesn't do anything but what I want to do. Like, one time I said I wanted ice cream in bed, so we went to the Scoop and got it at, like, ten o'clock at night!" Dori's eyes darted to her mother to see if she was in trouble for confessing this secret.

"Wow," said Sandy with a smile. "So you have a pretty special relationship with him?"

"Uh-huh. I do. Momma says I have him on my little finger. It means I'm kinda like his boss!" Dori nodded emphatically.

"Now, you said you could stay there before you were hurt. Dori, do you remember the night you were hurt?"

"Uh-huh," she said, looking down.

"Where were you?"

"For which part?" asked Dori, still not making eye contact.

"Let's start at the beginning. Were you at your house that night?"

"No. Mommy and Daddy ..." She turned to look for her parents. "They are sitting over there," she said, pointing. Laurie looked at Harold quickly, not sure how to react. Harold sat statuesquely, not making any movement except for with his hand with which he patted Laurie's knee in a manner intended to calm her.

"Okay. Go ahead, Dori. You were saying your mommy and daddy were what?" Sandy prompted her.

"Well, Mommy and Daddy had a Mardi Gras party." Her face wrinkled in contemplation as she paused. "I don't remember where. Is that okay?" Dori said, her little eyebrows arching in fear.

Sandy nodded her head yes.

"Okay. So me and Uncle Lee got to be together. So we went to eat at a place called Commander's Palace. Uncle Lee said that I was the only child there because I am different from regular kids. That's why he said he could take me to fancy-schmancy places like that. They even made my bananas foster at the table. They made it on fire!"

"Wow! Okay, Dori, so what did you do after dinner?"

"We rode on the streetcar. Mommy and Daddy don't really like riding on it, but Uncle Lee always says yes when I ask! But it doesn't go all the way to Uncle Lee's house, so we walked the rest of the way. But I like walking to Uncle Lee's, because Scoops is on the way there! Uncle Lee teases me about how I sleep better when I have ice cream. I reminded him that I was ready for a little ice cream before bed. Mommy and Daddy don't let me eat stuff that rots my teeth before bed, but ice cream before bed *always* happens at Uncle Lee's!"

"I see. What did you do after ice cream?"

"Um, well, I don't think I did anything. We got to Uncle Lee's house, I mean. I remember I brushed my teeth and stuff, and then Uncle Lee read me a story." Smiling, she continued. "Then, I got to get into a great big, ginormous bed! I could roll around for*ever* and not fall out of that bed!"

"How cool is that! Okay, is that bed in one of Uncle Lee's bedrooms?"

"Yes."

"Is it upstairs or downstairs?"

"It's up the stairs, like going this way." Dori moved her right hand as if it were sailing through the air.

"Do you remember if the windows were open?"

"Um, I don't know, Miss Sandy."

"That's okay. Did you eventually go to sleep?"

"Yes, but only for, like, a little while. Then I woke up." Dori looked down at her hands again.

"Where did you go when you woke up?"

"I went to Uncle Lee's room to see his clock."

"Why did you want to know what time it was?"

"My daddy was taking me to a party at the zoo, and I knew he was coming to get me early in the morning. I was worried I was missing it."

"Did you see the time?"

"Well, no, I couldn't tell what time it was on Uncle Lee's clock. So I went downstairs, because he has another one on the stove that I could tell the time better from. 'Member I told you about how that clock has the numbers on it already, instead of pointing to the numbers?"

"Do you remember the time, Dori?"

"No. But I remember seeing the stranger."

"Well, let's talk about that some. Where did you see the stranger?"

"He was standing by the back door."

"Do you remember what he looked like?"

"Yes."

The court reporter interrupted. "Judge, I simply cannot hear. She needs to speak at an audible level." Then she put back on her earphones, visibly aggravated.

The judge stared at her for a second before looking at Dori. "Hon, we are going to need you to speak as loud as you can because this nice lady here," he said, pointing at the obviously not very nice court reporter, "is typing what you say. Okay, now, carry on, Counselor."

Sandy looked at them both, wondering what was wrong with those two people. Were they not hugged enough as children? She turned her attention back to Dori.

"Now, Dori, you said you remember what he looked like?"

"Yes, ma'am."

"Do you see him here in the courtroom?"

Dori glanced around. "No."

Sandy paused, caught off guard, "Are you sure?"

Dori looked around again. "No, I don't, Miss Sandy."

Sandy just looked at Dori and at those innocent blue eyes peering up at her. Then it dawned on her! She walked back to her table and grabbed a photo of the defendant taken on the night he was arrested. After marking it as a State's exhibit, she approached Dori.

"Dori, do you recognize this man?"

Dori looked at the picture and then looked away, as if feeling a little ill. "That's him. That's the stranger. That's the one who ... who ..." Dori became teary-eyed.

"Dori, can you tell the judge what happened when you saw this man," Sandy said, pointing at the picture, "at Uncle Lee's back door?"

"He was waving at me." Dori shook her head sadly. "He was saying words, but I didn't understand him no matter how close I got." Dori paused, looking past Sandy into a blank space that was a sad memory. "I opened the door." Dori's eyes shot back to Sandy. "I opened the door, Miss Sandy. I wished I didn't, but I did. I opened the door."

"It's okay," Sandy said, reaching her hand across the witness box and placing it on top of Dori's. "What happened when you opened the door?" Sandy asked softly.

Sandy couldn't help herself; she had to glance back at the monster. Perhaps she expected him to be looking away. Perhaps she expected him to look angry or to be shaking his head feverishly in denial.

Whatever she had anticipated, she certainly didn't expect what she saw. Gurganus was leaning forward slightly in his chair, his elbows on the armrest and his hands meeting each other in the middle of his chest. His eyes stared intently at the child. He looked ... enthralled. He hung on every word that came out of that young child's mouth. His eyes smiled. Or was that pride? What was that look? It dawned on Sandy, and she gasped.

He's enjoying this! she thought. *That asshole is actually enjoying this.* She turned back to Dori, praying that the child hadn't noticed as well. But Dori had covered her little eyes. She continued through her tears to tell the gruesome story of the attack and rape. It was a gruesome story, indeed—and one that was such a turn-on for the monster.

127

Sandy could feel her stomach churning. She turned to look at Gurganus again. *Is this how he looked when I told my story? Is this what he thought while he saw me describe in brutal detail the abuse I endured? Is this his favorite part?*

She stared at him. Suddenly and without notice, Sandy could hear no more sounds. She couldn't hear Dori sobbing, she couldn't hear her description of that night. She didn't notice Mrs. Dauzat bury her face in her husband's neck so that Dori wouldn't see her cry. She couldn't hear the bailiff's newspaper's rattling. She couldn't hear Samuel clearing his throat.

She was trapped in a room with no noise. No noise and just his face. His hands grabbing at her. His scent filling her nostrils. And then she was gone. Just like that. Sandy was at the cabin, and then at the park, and then at dinner with her parents, laughing, the smell of her dad's cologne replacing the monster's stench. She was napping in a hammock. *Where was she, exactly? Lost in time somewhere? Lost in her own thoughts?*

Then a gentle tug on the arm of her suit jacket snapped her back. She looked down at the little hand tugging on her suit. And then her eyes went immediately to Dori's face. Dori's big blue eyes were wide and bright, still tearstained.

"What?" Sandy said, confused. "I'm sorry, what?"

Dori said, "Miss Sandy, you are going to get in big trouble," and she pointed to the judge. Sandy turned her attention to Judge Bryson.

"I'm sorry, Judge, what?" Sandy's face was confused. She was becoming anxious. Samuel looked amused.

"Ms. Morgan, please approach," Judge Bryson demanded. Sandy walked slowly to the judge's bench.

"Listen," he began, his voice hardly more than a stern whisper. "Isn't the subject matter disgusting enough without your constantly being distracted and lost in space? I will not tolerate any more trips to a land far, far away during this child's testimony. Do you understand, Ms. Morgan?!"

Sandy just stared blankly at Judge Bryson. "Judge, I don't even know where to start. I apologize. I guess I just sort of daydreamed, I don't know. But, anyway, it won't happen again."

The judge's face softened a little. He said, "Good. Now, let's continue and get this kid off the stand before we are all traumatized beyond repair."

Sandy turned and walked back toward her tiny witness. She looked nervous, like her best friend had been sent to time-out.

Sandy winked at Dori, and the tension on Dori's face eased a bit. "All right, Dori, let's finish up, okay?"

"Okay," Dori said, although her apprehensive tone made it clear that she had no idea what "finishing up" might entail.

"Dori, can you remind us? What was the last part of the story you had told us?" Sandy prayed that the child remembered.

"Remember, I was telling about the angel that took my mind away."

"Ah, yes," Sandy responded, as if this jogged her memory. "What is the very next thing you remember?"

"Well, I woke up in the hospital. And my mommy and daddy were very happy because I was asleep for a long time."

"Dori, you did a great job." Then, turning to the judge, Sandy said, "I have no further questions."

The judge visibly sighed. "Good. Mr. Samuel, do you have any questions?"

Samuel said, "In fact, I do."

As he jotted down one last note, Sandy took a good look at him. This would be interesting. What could he ask her? He had to walk a tightrope, after all. You can't be too aggressive with such a young witness. You can't ask about her sexual past and try to make it look like she was a willing participant. So, what would he ask?

Samuel stood and, much to Sandy's surprise, spoke to Dori in a softer tone than she had thought him capable of.

"Good morning, Miss Dori. You look lovely in that dress."

Dori smiled meekly and responded with a quiet, "Thank you."

"Miss Dori, do you know this man?" Samuel pointed to Gurganus. Dori shook her head no.

"Can you say it out loud for us?" he asked, smiling.

"No, I don't know him."

"Very good. Now, Miss Dori, is this the man who did those hurtful things to you?"

Dori looked confused, but she shook her head while saying no.

"In fact, have you ever even seen this man before?" he asked, still pointing.

"No." Dori glanced at Sandy.

"Thank you, Miss Dori," he said, smiling at the child. Then he turned his attention to the judge. "I have no further questions for the child."

Judge Bryson didn't even look up when he said, "Redirect?"

Sandy again showed Dori the mug shot from the night of Gurganus's arrest and asked Dori if that was the man who hurt her. Dori assured her that it was.

CHAPTER 15

August 11, Evening

WHY CAN'T WE INVEST IN CALLER ID HERE? SANDY THOUGHT, TRYING to decide whether or not to answer her ringing office phone. *Nine-thirty at night. Hm, probably okay,* she thought as she picked up the phone.

"Sandy Morgan," she said into the receiver.

"Still there, honey?" came the soft voice of her father.

"Hey, Daddy-O!" Though tired, she was happy to hear her father's voice. Her conservative tan jacket had long ago been strewn across the back of the chair that sits opposite her desk, revealing a tighter (and much less conservative) white blouse. Tan heels lay next to her credenza, patiently waiting to go home. "Yes, still here. I'm sure there are only one or two witnesses tomorrow, so I'm working on my closing arguments."

"How did today go? How was the little girl?"

"Dori? Well, she did a great job, considering that she is five and that that monster stared at her the whole time." Then, considering the question more seriously, she said, "Thing is, though, she couldn't identify him in the courtroom."

"Why?" her dad asked, concerned.

"Well, he looks so different. Longer beard now, looks all scruffy. In his arrest picture, he has his hair pulled back, things like that." Sandy sighed. "I don't think it's that big of a deal, though. She identified the mug shot. I was still able to get the fingerprint evidence in. Clearly, it was him," Sandy said with resolve.

She continued her summary by saying, "We also had Lee Lawson, the guy who was babysitting her; Leila Mayer, who is the child's doctor; Seth Tyler, who was the reporting officer; Bradley Curtis, my detective; and Shane Crosby, the forensic analyst."

"Let me guess, the detective did a great job. An excellent job. The best job any detective has ever done."

"Dad!"

"Fine, what did the babysitter say?" her dad asked quietly.

"Wow, Dad, it was pretty gripping testimony," she answered, her voice softening. "The entire courtroom was silent. Just terrible. He described finding her on the lawn, the blood, and her screams. He said there were no words, just a deep guttural scream. It was just wretched, Dad."

"Poor baby," her father said as he sighed.

"This is a pretty prominent guy, too. But you could tell that he will never have another peaceful night's sleep. He just hasn't forgiven himself. Half of his testimony was through angry, gritted teeth. Of course, there wasn't a dry eye in the room. That is, until the idiot got up to cross-examine him."

Her father interrupted. "What idiot?"

"Samuel. You remember, Robert Samuel?"

"Ah, yes," he responded, "definitely an idiot."

"I know, right? Well, to his credit, he was able to get Lee to admit that the defendant had done some work in his home. But in my redirect, I also got him to testify to two important things. First, the work the defendant had done was yard work, which would not require him to use tape, and second, even if he had used the tape,

Lee hadn't seen or used that tape in months and certainly had not left it on the kitchen table."

Sandy paused, contemplating. "I just don't see it, Dad. I don't see how I could lose. I think this one is in the bag."

Her father sighed. "I hope so, honey—and then maybe you will sleep in peace."

Sandy couldn't respond. She felt terrible about concealing the truth from her father, not that she was considering confiding in him. She knew that this secret was her own and that she would take it to her grave.

"By the way," he continued, "I have a light day tomorrow. I thought I would swing by. You know, watch your closing and give you some moral support."

Sandy's head started swirling. What if he recognized Gurganus? She thought quickly. "Oh, no need, Dad. There is just one witness left, the little girl's mom. She will be short. Just testifying about the damages done to her daughter, the coma, etc. I doubt the defendant will testify. I, uh, well, I might get nervous if you are there."

There. She said her lie, and then she waited. Nothing. There was a long pause before her dad finally said, "Okay. Well, if you change your mind."

He sighed. She hated disappointing him, but there was no going back. She had to carry this burden alone.

Changing the subject, she asked, "So, any update on this crazy weather?"

CHAPTER 16

August 12, Morning

"THERE WILL ONLY BE A SHORT RECESS BEFORE CLOSING ARGUMENTS. As you are all aware, the parish has issued a tropical storm warning for a storm expected to hit this afternoon. In fact, the winds have already picked up, it is raining, they are recommending evacuating, yada yada, and we all need to get out of here. I expect our two learned counselors to make their arguments short and to the point. No fluff. Seriously. This isn't a jury trial, so no need to dance around and put on an act. I know the facts and have listened attentively, but it's time to wrap this up and head out of town."

And with that, the judge told them to enjoy the short lunch break and be back ready to give their closing arguments at 1:30—a whole hour and fifteen minutes later.

The courtroom cleared. As it did, Sandy flipped furiously through her notes and continued working on the outline for her closing arguments. She wanted to remind the judge about the testimony of all the key witnesses.

She was relieved that she had taken so much time to work on her outline the night before, especially since today's testimony would consist of what Sandy considered to be standard questions and answers.

Sandy walked to the window. She stared out onto the busy street outside the courthouse. The sky was gray and darkening quickly. Sandy watched a nervous woman trying to hold onto her papers and skirt at the same time while walking down the courthouse steps. She concluded that the winds had, indeed, picked up.

Her mind began to wander. It was dark. She saw his thick hands. She could feel them pulling at her, holding her down. The smell of smoke filling her nostrils and choking her. She shook her head as if to shake off the feeling, and she wondered whether or not he would steal her thoughts anymore once he was in prison forever. Would she still get these feelings? She was tired. Exhausted. Beat up.

"So, is it done?"

His voice echoed across the room, startling her. She turned to see her father leaning against the courtroom door.

"How long have you been there?"

Ignoring her question, he asked again, "What was the outcome?" this time more sternly. He moved in a little closer, his shoes making a solid pounding sound that echoed rhythmically throughout the empty space. His dark gray suit was perfectly tailored; his briefcase was of fine leather; one of his hands was in his pocket. He had crossed the courtroom, opened the gate that separated the audience from the front, and came to a stop just in front of her prosecutor's table.

"I don't know," she said, shrugging solemnly. "I have to deliver my closing in about half an hour." Then, turning back to the window, she asked with aggravation, "Are you checking up on me?"

"Actually," he said, his voice softening, "more like checking in with you. I figured this trial was over or would be over soon, and I wanted to know what you were doing after."

"After?" she said, her eyebrows arching in confusion as she glanced over her shoulder at her father. *Funny,* she thought, *I didn't consider after. Is there an after?* She turned back toward the window.

She felt his hands on her shoulders and his head coming to rest next to hers. She closed her eyes and breathed in deeply, smelling his cologne.

He sighed deeply, too. Sensing the need to change the subject, he began. "Well, your mother and I are going to stay home, despite the weather. It's only a tropical storm, after all. Mainly a rain and wind event, they are saying on the news. Why don't you join us?"

Sandy didn't respond. She was fighting back tears.

"I'll make you tea."

Still no response.

"Soup?" he tried again.

"Lick?" he asked, upping the ante.

She turned to him and smiled. "Okay, Dad. I'll think about it."

He smiled back, knowing that this was about as close as he was going to get to a yes.

"All right, honey. I'll let you get back to work," he said. He kissed her forehead and turned to leave. "Me," he said over his shoulder, "I'm heading home early. I'm going to beat the rain!" he said optimistically.

She watched as he made it to the back of the empty courtroom, at which point he turned abruptly and said, "Sandy, I do love you, honey. I really do."

Sandy nodded as if saying, "I know," before turning back toward the window, lest he see her tears.

CHAPTER 17

August 12, Afternoon

"ALL RISE," ANNOUNCED THE BAILIFF, MAKING NO EFFORT TO HIDE his grumpiness, which was the result of his having to return for the closing arguments rather than get a head start on his weekend.

Judge Bryson came out with a fishing magazine in one hand and a cup of coffee in the other. *I wonder how much of these arguments he'll hear while he studies spearfishing?* Sandy pondered, feeling a little dejected.

"All right, folks. Let's get this done. No extra editorials. Remember, make it short and to the point. Ms. Morgan, you're up," he said as he leaned back in his chair to get comfortable, stretched a little, and sighed as he reached for his coffee cup.

Sandy grabbed her legal pad and began to approach the podium. She flipped her notes to the first page, took a deep breath, and began.

"Seven witnesses. Seven witnesses comprised of one doctor, three policemen, a parent, a friend, and a small child. Seven witnesses to explain to this honorable court the brutal and horrendous rape of and abuse endured by a five-year-old baby on February twenty-third. Seven witnesses who swore to God and then looked you in the eye while pointing to the person who did it." Sandy stepped away from the podium and moved closer to the defendant, pointing at him emphatically.

"That night in February has long since passed. That night when this defendant pulled young Dori out of the comfort of a warm and loving home and landed her in the cold, wet grass, bleeding, bruised, scared, and torn. That night, this defendant took her innocence, took her voice, broke her will, and then stripped her of any chance to have a family of her own. For Dori, that night will survive past today and will live in her forever.

"I as a prosecutor, you as a judge, and the members of our city and parish are all obligated today. We are obligated to protect the innocent. We are obligated to enforce our laws, which were written to protect the innocent. One undisputed and incontrovertible fact that will remain consistent at the end of the day is this: an innocent child cries out for our protection. Our burden is simple, as the defendant left a trail of breadcrumbs right to his doorstep. We must give him just punishment, or at least as just a punishment as possible within the confines of our laws.

"In deciding what that just punishment will be, let us reflect on the testimony of the seven voices that were brave enough to speak out loud.

"First, the court heard from Lee Lawson. The court cannot possibly deny that Mr. Lawson was credible and honest. Mr. Lawson explained to the court his involvement with the Dauzat family. He has known them practically his whole life—and certainly for Dori's whole life. He is her godfather. He was there the day she was born. That night forever changed Dori's life, but it forever changed Mr. Lawson's life, too.

"The court can imagine how awful this night was. He puts the child to bed. He reads her a story. He checks on her on his way to bed. He awakes to find her gone. The sheer terror that she is not there. The frantic search for her. The way he found her, battered and torn on the lawn.

"Mr. Lawson also explained to the court that he had hired Mr. Gurganus to do some work on his home. But that work was yard work, and it was over two years ago, by the best of his recollection.

"Now, Mr. Samuel would have you believe that the fingerprints found on the tape—the tape that matched the tape on Dori's body—matched his client's because of the work the defendant did at Lee Lawson's home. He would have this court believe that one uses tape when mowing grass. I submit to you that this argument is illogical at best and obnoxious at worst.

"Next, the court heard from our expert. Connor Lewis is the chief forensic analyst, and he confirmed that the fingerprints found inside Mr. Lawson's home were, in fact, those of this defendant.

"You heard from Dori's doctor, Leila Mayer, who described in detail and with medical certainty that the child was indeed raped, beaten, and mentally abused—to the point that she went into a coma. Dori was bruised and battered, and suffered internal tearing so severe that she will never have children of her own.

"You heard from the reporting officer, Seth Tyler, the first to arrive on the scene. This is a seasoned officer who had to pause a moment to keep his own emotions under control as he told you the story of walking into the Lawson home that night and seeing Mr. Lawson cradle Dori as if nothing in the world could tear them apart. He told you that the scene didn't seem altered or staged. He told you about that moment—that one moment when Dori was taken from Lee Lawson. He also described that baby's raw reaction.

"Next, you heard from Detective Curtis. He explained in detail the process he used for collecting the evidence and how his investigation pointed in only one direction: that of the defendant.

"You heard from Laurie, who described to you the absolute horror she felt upon getting the call telling her that her five-year-old baby was severely raped, beaten, and abandoned for dead.

"Finally, you heard from Dori. Dori. The bravest five-year-old in New Orleans.

"I will end this trial just as it began: I will remind the court about Dori. Dori will never smell smoke again and not think of Bruce Gurganus. Dori will never be in a kitchen alone without being afraid. Dori will not set off to college like the happy-go-lucky child she should be, but will instead spend the rest of her life guarded and isolated. Dori will never know the free way in which a man and a woman can love each other because she will always have, in the scars he left on her body and in her heart, a barrier against intimacy.

"Dori Dauzat, age five, will carry Bruce Gurganus's stench on her for the rest of her life. She will dream of him and she will hate him. And fight him as she might in her dreams, he will be there again and again, pulling at her, holding her down, violating her.

"Dori Dauzat, age five, deserved better than that. I implore this honorable court to protect all of the children out there like Dori from this brutal and vicious defendant. I implore this court to stand up for Dori and order that justice be served. I implore this court to render the only possible verdict: the defendant is guilty as charged."

Sandy picked up her yellow legal pad, flipped the pages to the front, and took a step back from the podium. She felt that she still had so much to say, and yet she had said it all. She paused there, unmoving, and clenched her notes to her chest. Judge Bryson was staring at her. For a split second, she thought she saw a flash of pity in his eyes.

From behind her and to the left at the defendant's table, a slow, loud noise interrupted the silence. Sandy turned her head sharply to see Mr. Samuel standing behind the defendant's table, next to his client. With the rest of his body as still as a statue, he was clapping his hands. The sound was slow, methodical, and piercing. It echoed across the nearly empty courtroom, its harsh sound slapping Sandy across her face with each thick and bold strike.

From the corner of her eye, she could see the movement of Lee Lawson as he began to stand, and then the quick, strong hands of Harold Dauzat pulling him down and holding him tightly.

Judge Bryson interrupted, shaking his head. "All right, all right. Enough of that, Mr. Samuel!"

The Southern drawl came out heavy and thick as Samuel said, "Why, I do apologize to the court, but that was a lovely, heartrending, and Emmy Award–winning oration if I've ever heard one," he said, his hands clenched together over his heart and his eyes never leaving Sandy's.

Her eyes darted away. She was uncomfortable and suddenly nervous. Was it enough? Had she said enough? All the hours she had invested, all the time she had put in, all the years she had spent waiting, without even knowing that she was waiting. It came down to this last argument, and there sat Samuel. He was confident, smug, and sarcastic to the point that Sandy felt the fear from her own childhood rearing its ugly, abused head. She reacted in the only way that she could. She moved quickly to her seat. The clanging of her dropped pen sounded throughout the courtroom. Her chair screeched out its reluctance as the wood scraped across the floor as she pulled it away from the desk.

She glanced up to see the judge and Samuel staring at her. The judge's face showed a look of pity. Samuel's countenance was one of dominance. She glared back at him, her anxiety having been replaced by her defiance.

"Problem is, of course, is that it has no foundation in fact. A small point that the young counselor seems to have forgotten is necessary," Samuel continued. Finally, turning his eyes to the judge, he asked, "May I proceed, Your Honor?"

The judge nodded to him and gave Samuel his familiar "Let's get on with it" wave. Then he motioned to the bailiff to come closer, and he held up his coffee cup. The bailiff, not at all amused about being the coffee boy, huffed and walked out of the room, coming back moments later with the refill and then taking his seat near the base of the judge's bench, where he resumed reading the sports section of the newspaper without giving a mere glance at the courtroom. *Some protector*, Sandy thought.

In the meantime, Samuel approached the podium. His gait was slow and confident; his hands, empty. When he reached to podium, he gave his client a quick wink client before he resumed speaking.

"May it please the court?"

The judge nodded yes as the court reporter made no effort to hide her yawn.

"I've sat here for two days. Two days of my life taken from me that I will never get back." He hung his head low and shook it slowly, as if in some kind of distress. "I listened to the famous seven witnesses, Your Honor. But unlike the State, I did not romanticize what they said." Raising a finger in the air, he said, "Instead, I listened to hear the key elements of the crime."

Then, dramatically hitting his fist on the podium, he said, in a voice that was raised but not quite yelling, "I listened for the proof."

Regaining his composure, he continued. "What happened to that baby is sad." He shook his head and looked down solemnly. "It's tragic. We all want the guilty party to pay," he said, shrugging. "But, just as it would be a travesty of justice if the person who committed this crime did not pay for it, it would be just as great a travesty if an innocent man paid for a crime he didn't commit." Samuel paused here.

"So, before we go getting all excited," he said while striking a dramatic and intentional pose, his left hand holding onto to his left lapel and his right hand raised shoulder height and moving with his every word, "let's talk about some of the things that Ms. Morgan forgot to remind the court of."

He continued. "Witness number one: good ole Mister Lawson. Oh, he's clean-shaven and speaks nicely. Told you what a brilliant architect he is and how he loved the victim's family. Heck, Judge, he painted himself as a perfect Boy Scout, now, didn't he?" Samuel paused carefully before raising his voice and saying, "But his fingerprints were on the tape! This is a man who is still single, who has never been married, and who is living a lifestyle straight out of *Lifestyles of the Rich and Famous!*"

Then, using one of his long fingers, he paused and traced the edge of the podium and expertly feigned confusion as he said, "Seems strange to me that parents would choose as a sitter a man accused of raping a girl in high school. I personally can't say I find it prudent to do so." Samuel shook his head back and forth in mock sorrow. "In fact," he continued, "I fear that the Dauzats' poor parenting decision has left this child terrorized and injured."

"Your Honor!" Sandy jumped from her seat, her face red and flushed with anger.

"Miss Morgan," the judge responded, motioning with his hand for her to sit. "Listen, you two. Has today not been long enough? There is no jury. The courtroom is practically empty. The only one here to impress is me—and, frankly, I'm over it. I am unimpressed," he said, stressing the last word and making quotation marks in the air with two fingers of each of his hands. "So, please, before this storm blows us all away, can we get on with it already?"

Samuel put his hand over his heart and nodded at the judge as if pledging to do just that. Then he continued.

"What I do know, Your Honor, is that this child was found in the arms of Lee Lawson. Found at his house. Found with her blood on him. Then this man, this unmarried man accused of rape, was allowed to go to the hospital and tell the child whatever he wanted. Her parents still allowed this man to be alone with their child as she lay in a hospital bed and recovered. He had weeks to speak to that child before she finally spoke to the detectives. That man had nothing to add to this trial—except making himself look like the guilty party."

Samuel had now moved in front of the podium and was pacing back and forth. *Damn, he's good*, thought Sandy. *Good thing this is a judge trial.*

"Number two and three," he continued. "Well, Officer Seth Tyler ... that was just a formality. Just an officer reporting what we all know. That injured child was being held by Lee Lawson, and he

143

wouldn't give her up. Then there is Detective Curtis. I agree with my young opposing counselor: this detective worked as hard as he could. He made up his mind that the rich architect could not possibly have done it and set about to prove that poor Mr. Gurganus did! It was a witch hunt, I tell you! He didn't even attempt to find another suspect. He simply decided that Mr. Gurganus was guilty, and then he closed the case. He halfheartedly and sloppily gathered the evidence and then gave it to the next law enforcement officer, Connor Lewis.

"Now, Connor Lewis—that was interesting testimony. Ms. Morgan harps on the fact that the tape had Mr. Gurganus's fingerprints on it and downplays the fact that it also had Lee Lawson's! Once again, back to Lee Lawson!

"The State also produced the child's doctor, Leila Mayer. Fine, there is no argument that this child was battered and, in many ways, changed forever. But this court cannot make its decision based on emotion or based on the damages! You must base it on guilt beyond a reasonable doubt.

"The fifth witness is the child's mother. While her testimony was sad, she wasn't there when her child was victimized. She can't tell this court who committed the crime any more than this bailiff can," he said, pointing at the bailiff, who raised his eyes above the paper and then went right back to reading.

"Finally, and tragically, the State put this poor child on the stand. Heartbreaking for all of us. But I asked her several times—heck, the State asked her—and at the end of the day, she could not identify my client as the man who hurt her. That's it. Case closed. She simply could not identify him.

"Your Honor, my client wanted a judge trial because we knew how hard this case would be. When a jury sees a hurt child, they want someone to pay, and rightfully so. We couldn't risk that they would act on emotion. That's why we chose you. We are confident that your understanding of the law, combined with the fact that the

State must prove guilt beyond a reasonable doubt, would lead you to only one possible outcome.

"At the end of the day, you have a child whose identification of a mug shot of a man who did a traumatic thing to her is not reliable because it was made weeks later, and she failed to identify him in person here in the courtroom. The only other real evidence you have is a fingerprint on tape that could have been there for months. This is simply not enough to prove guilt beyond a reasonable doubt. There can only be one outcome. Not guilty. Not guilty. Not guilty."

Samuel walked toward his seat, giving a nod to his client before outstretching his hand. Gurganus shook his hand and smiled weakly. Sandy took a little pleasure in the fact that Gurganus appeared nervous.

"All right, I believe that concludes the case," Judge Bryson began.

"Wait," Sandy interrupted, "my final summation."

"Is it necessary? What part do you think I didn't understand?"

"Well, Your Honor, the identification from Dori," she began.

"I got it. She didn't identify him here but did in the arrest photo. Got it. Is that all?"

"Um … I suppose so." Sandy floundered for a better response.

"Great." Judge Bryson was clear that he was done hearing from them. "I need a quick recess. Court is adjourned for five minutes." After striking the gavel, he fumbled down the couple of stairs and into his chambers.

Sandy was still standing, a little stunned. It was over. It was done. Now it was just the ruling. She could hear Samuel talking but could only make out the occasional word. She heard *appeal, confident,* and something about the defendant's jail cell. She wasn't sure she wanted to hear any more. Of course, if they were talking about an appeal, then maybe she should feel more confident. Sandy felt herself nudged on the shoulder and turned.

"What do you think?" It was Harold.

"It's always hard to say. I feel confident," Sandy said, sounding the opposite of confident. "What's your impression?"

Harold hung his head and shrugged his shoulders, sitting back close to his wife. Laurie patted his leg and said, "I think it went really well. I think he will be in prison for the rest of his life." Her words would have been more comforting if they had possessed any trace of conviction.

Lee, who at this point hadn't even looked at Sandy, finally turned to her and said, "This is bullshit."

"Lee," Laurie interrupted.

"No, Laurie," he continued, his voice rising. "This is utter bullshit. That disgusting animal over there"—he was now over normal conversation tones and border line yelling, and pointing at Gurganus—"is a sick, perverted rapist." The bailiff stood up and walked nervously and quietly toward the center of the courtroom. Lee stood and turned his whole body toward Gurganus, who looked straight ahead as if he hadn't heard a word he was saying.

"He should be in jail where he will be gang-raped daily when the other prisoners realize he is a child rapist." Then, suddenly turning his anger on Sandy, Lawson practically screamed, "But you motherfuckers screwed up this case so fucking bad that this disgusting excuse for a human is going to walk!"

"Lee!" Laurie grabbed his arm and tried to calm him.

Harold pleaded with him, "Dude, chill. Stop. You are in a courtroom."

Then, as if they had all been saved by the bell, the door to the judge's chambers opened and the judge unaware of anything happening in the courtroom, climbed onto the bench, ready to rule. Sandy held her breath.

"I have sat through two days of evidence. I have carefully listened. It is not an easy task to have someone's life in your hands. In one sense, I have the Dauzat family. They only want the best for their daughter, and they want justice served to the man who forever changed her life.

On the other hand, I have the defendant, Gurganus, who is entitled to a fair trial and to a not-guilty verdict unless the evidence shows beyond a reasonable doubt that he committed the crime. Reasonable doubt cannot be random or fleeting, and it can't be taken lightly. This system is one I strongly believe in, as it is better to let a guilty man go free than to take away the freedom of an innocent man. Though, I suppose, if you are the Dauzats, the victims of a violent crime, you may feel that the system should be different.

"Having said that and having given careful consideration to the evidence and testimony, I hereby find the defendant not guilty."

Sandy could hear a gasp. Had it come from her? No. She turned and looked behind her to find the blank stares of Harold and Laurie Dauzat and Lee Lawson. She jerked her head toward the defendant when she heard a slapping sound, which turned out to be Samuel's slapping Gurganus on the back. Then she heard commotion behind her.

Sandy turned in time to see Lee Lawson coming through the gate with Harold holding onto him and pulling him backward. The bailiff was there in moments, although to Sandy, everything appeared to be happening in slow motion. She couldn't seem to hear the noise, although she could clearly see people's mouths moving. Harold and the bailiff managed to get Lee Lawson all the way to the back of the courtroom and through the heavy doors. Sandy could hear the scuffle and the muffled yelling from the hallway.

Laurie Dauzat sat unmoving, staring ahead.

Sandy looked at the defense's table as the judge said, "Mr. Gurganus, we have some documents for you to sign before your release. After that, your business with this court is complete."

Sandy stared at Gurganus as he asked about collecting his belongings from the jail and posed other questions that seemed ridiculous to her. Samuel answered but kept checking his watch. Case over, check cashed, ready to go.

Harold reentered the courtroom. He gently grabbed Laurie's arm, as if to help her to stand. She looked at him blankly, speaking no words.

Harold glanced at Sandy as he escorted Laurie out of the long row. She wanted to say something, to yell something. Her mouth moved a little, but no words came out. Harold just nodded at Sandy. It was a "You tried your best but lost" nod. It was a nod that cut her wide open, as if she had been pierced with a machete. And then they were gone—out the back of the courtroom and gone forever. Sandy knew she failed them. Her fault or not, she had failed.

She looked back at Gurganus as his handcuffs were being removed. She found Samuel standing in front of her with his hand outstretched. *He wants to shake my hand?* she thought.

She took his hand, staring at each of their hands as they shook and not making eye contact. She could hear him saying something but couldn't bring herself to listen. Then he, too, was gone. Gurganus began walking with the bailiff toward the jail entrance on the side of the courtroom. Off to collect his things and sign out, Sandy supposed. Just before disappearing through the door, he glanced back at Sandy and winked. Her eyebrows arched in surprise. Then he was gone.

She looked around and realized they were all gone. Literally. She was there alone. Alone with the file marked *State of Louisiana v. Bruce Gurganus* and several small manila folders marked the same way. She looked at the floor where the empty brown box sat. She sat in her chair at the prosecutor's table. Several minutes later, the bailiff returned.

"Miss, I need to lock up. You best be getting home now. Storm's coming."

Sandy gathered her file and stuffed it into the brown box. Looking at it with disgust and dismissing the thought of abandoning it right there, she reluctantly picked it up and turned to leave. Sitting in the last row was her detective. She walked through the gate and approached the back doors. Curtis stood.

"Sandy," he said softly, reaching for her.

Sandy pulled back. She looked at him sadly and then shook her head no. She couldn't speak. She wasn't ready to be comforted.

Curtis followed her out of the courtroom and watched her as she walked down the long corridor to the district attorney's building. He didn't follow after her. He knew she needed her space.

The front doors to the courthouse swung open under Sandy's firm push. The winds had already picked up, blowing her skirt about her knees and her hair into her eyes. She noticed that the courthouse steps were empty as she practically ran for the safety of her office.

It wasn't the weather she was running from; it was the tears. She was running for a safe place, a place where she could scream.

She made it to her office building. It was already dark and locked. She swiped her card to unlock the door, straining slightly to push open the heavy glass without dropping the box. Sandy darted up the stairs, box in hand, and down the long, dark hallway to the haven of her office. She swung the door open wide. She dropped the box on the floor just inside, slammed the door shut, and locked it.

She pressed her back against the door and reached to flip on the light without looking for the switch. The light came on silently and glowed yellow.

The office looked just as it had when she last left it. She could see her half bottle of water sitting by the keyboard. Her sweater was still hanging half on and half off the back of her desk chair.

Sandy began to wander around the little space aimlessly. A stack of exhibits leaned against the wall just as they had earlier. Two old but comfortable chairs sat in front of her desk. Stacks of files for Monday's hearings had been placed there by the paralegal sometime during the day while Sandy was at trial. Several messages were stuck on the top of her full inbox.

Everything was the same. *Nothing different,* she thought. Yet everything felt different to Sandy.

It's me … it's me. I guess I just … failed, she thought sadly. The moment the thought entered her mind, her anger took over. Her face reddened and her chest felt tight. The need to fight, to strike out, had hit her so quickly that she had no time to reason with herself.

"I *failed*," she yelled. She ran for her desk. With one swipe of an angry arm, she flung the files across the room. She ripped the books from the shelf and took aim at her chair.

She kicked it—hard. She had little balance and no control, so when the heel of her shoe caught the edge of her desk, Sandy quickly and unexpectedly lost her balance. She began a most ungraceful plummet. As she fell, her jacket caught onto the handle of the desk drawer, causing the top of her body and the bottom of her body to go in different directions. Sandy landed on top of the toppled chair.

She didn't move for a moment. The shock of having fell and landed so hard and awkwardly led her to perform a quick injury assessment. She wasn't hurt, but she was still broken.

Sandy began to sob. She lay there, her body sprawled in different directions, and let herself lose control for a minute. Finally, as Sandy began to untangle herself from her tears, she saw an object made of black metal sitting in her slightly open drawer. All at once, she knew what to do.

Sandy slowly opened the drawer. The gun her father had given to her for purposes of personal protection sat there, cheering her on. "I'm going to protect myself, all right," she said out loud. "And every other kid out there."

Her rain jacket and umbrella were in the corner under some books and strewn papers. *Perfect,* she thought. Sandy grabbed the gun and walked to the corner. She put on the jacket, buttoning every button. She slipped the gun into her pocket and tucked the umbrella under her arm. Grabbing her keys and the brown box, she locked her office door and began walking confidently to the staircase.

She was calm. In fact, it occurred to her just how calm she was as she devised her plan. It was simple. Walk to the jail just behind the building, and shoot him when he walked out. She would serve justice fast and without explanation. Then she would get in her car and leave. Simple.

She pushed open the heavy door of the office building and walked out. The parking lot for the district attorney's office sat between her office and the jail. Sandy paused for a second to evaluate where she should stand. The winds had picked up some since she had gone into the office; the occasional raindrop fought for attention. She walked toward her car. The rain began coming down in strange sheets of light. After a suddenly heavy downpour, it was back to light rain. Sandy opened the umbrella.

The streets were virtually empty. Sporadically, she saw a person run across the parking lot or dart into a building. For the most part, she knew that she would go unseen. Sandy shoved the brown box into her trunk and jumped in her car to watch the jail entrance.

She watched for what seemed like hours. She watched as other sheriffs made their way to the jail for emergency storm duty. She watched as the rain came and went and the winds picked up and then died again. She watched her windshield wipers make shadows dance across her dash. It felt like she was watching the grass grow.

Then it happened. She saw him. She rolled her window down. Would she have a clear shot from here? Could she pull it off?

Gurganus paused as he walked out, taking a deep breath of fresh air and looking around as if deciding whether to go left or right. Sandy raised her gun and pointed it out the car window, trying to steady her hand.

Between the parked cars and Gurganus's movement, Sandy was afraid she'd miss. "Damn it," she said, and jumped out of her car. She opened the umbrella and pulled it as far down as she could to cover her face. Slipping her gun into her right pocket, she walked quickly toward him.

She could see him lighting a cigarette and choosing the direction opposite from her. The soft puff of cigarette smoke came from in front of him, although he had turned so that all she could see was the back of his body. He walked with no certain destination. *He has no idea he is making his last walk,* she thought.

151

She reached the edge of the parking lot and stepped onto the sidewalk. Her heels made the click-clack sound that many women are used to hearing when they walk across pavement. She began crossing the street just as he cleared the cars.

She pulled the gun from her pocket and tried to steady it while maintaining her quick walking pace. She stepped onto the other sidewalk and dropped the umbrella. She stopped, extending her arms forward and locking them. He was still walking straight ahead, but away from her. He hadn't heard her shoes. He hadn't heard the click of her gun as she cocked it. He wouldn't have time to hear the shot before it took his life. She took a deep breath and aimed at the back of his head.

CHAPTER 18

HAD YOU ASKED HER AT THE EXACT TIME THAT IT HAD HAPPENED, Sandy would not have ever been able to tell you what it was that hit her. It was like a deer hitting a car. It was so fast and strong that it had knocked her right off her feet.

She found herself falling under his weight, catching a quick glimpse of Curtis Bradley's face in her confusion. He had come in from her left side, performing some sort of high school tackle move that sent Sandy sprawling into the street.

The hand in which she held her gun hit the edge of the blacktop. She inadvertently let go of the weapon. She could distinctly hear the heavy metal sound as the gun bounced across the pavement, coming to land in the middle of the street.

She could see Bradley's mouth moving, forming angry, pleading words, but she could not discern them. She had landed hard and painfully on her right side and then had immediately turned her entire body toward the middle of the street to desperately reach out for her gun.

She had one mission. One vision. She must reach her gun. The pavement was hard and wet; she could feel it tearing at the skin on the side of her legs. She could hear material ripping, but she didn't look because she didn't care which part of her suit was causing the noise.

She rolled onto her stomach and clamored to get away from him, reaching and pulling as she did so. She could feel him, heavy, on the back of her legs.

"No!" Bradley yelled through clenched teeth as he clutched at her and pulled her to himself. His grip was alternately strong and weak because the soft drizzle had made her slippery and hard to hold onto.

Finally hearing his voice, she yelled over her shoulder as she kicked and scratched at him. "Let me go. Stop! Let me go! Let me finish this!"

Realizing that she was making no headway in reaching her weapon, she turned from her stomach to her backside. She accomplished the task of sitting up, using her arms to prop herself while Bradley held on to her scraped-up legs.

She kicked him hard. She focused all of the strength she had into the hardest double-legged kick to the chest she could muster. Bradley held on tighter. She began to sob as she repeatedly kicked him. The impact of her kicks grew weaker as his hold on her grew stronger.

"You know I can't let you do this." Bradley fought to stop her—to save her from herself.

Sandy shrieked profanity at him and tried again to kick him away.

"Sandy, I can't let you do this. Please, you have to listen to me." His arms moved in one quick gesture from her legs to her waist. He lay halfway across her legs and tried to get her to look him in the eyes. He wanted her to see that he was serious. He wanted to try to find her amid that frantic, lost gaze on her face.

Sandy looked back over her shoulder for Gurganus, only to see him making his way around the corner, about to disappear. She sobbed and hollered.

"Let me go! You bastard, you have no right to stop me! It's my choice! It's *my choice!* Let me go!" Sandy used her arms and legs to try to get away. Her skirt was now raised almost completely over her buttocks. One of her heels was missing; her knees were badly scraped. She was desperate.

Bradley let go of her waist only to grab her shoulders. He pulled her to himself there on the ground. "I understand," he said. He started speaking softly into her hair. "I understand, Sandy. Please, let me help you. You will lose everything. You are risking everything. Please, don't give him the rest of your life."

She pulled away from him as if he had struck her across the face. "I have no life!" she barked back. She dug her fingernails into his arms and strained under his hold. She gained a little freedom and kicked at him again, this time loosening both of her arms and one leg from his grip.

He still had hold of one slippery leg, but as she flipped onto her arms and legs and crawled toward the street, she freed herself completely. He sat on the street, winded and still protesting.

But before Sandy could reach the gun, a distinct sound stopped them both in their tracks. They heard a gunshot in the very near distance. Sandy, only half standing, turned back toward Bradley. She was staring at him as if asking, *Did you hear that?*

Bradley instinctively jumped to his knees and raised his right hand to her in a "stop" gesture, telling her to keep quiet. They were both very still for a couple more moments. Then Bradley unsnapped his holster and rose to his feet in a crouching stand.

Looking like he had been in the fight of his life, he began making his way toward the street corner. His slacks were torn near the ankle, he was wet, and he had a button or two missing from his shirt. He turned back to Sandy and put a finger to his lips to ask her to remain hushed. As he got closer to the corner, he again turned back and motioned for Sandy to stay where she was.

Sandy suddenly realized that she was still in the middle of the street. She took a quick look around for her shoe, which she found half in a water drain, and slipped it on her foot. She then grabbed her gun. She placed the gun back into her jacket pocket.

Without giving it much thought, she began to follow Bradley around the corner. She crept quietly toward the place where Bradley had just made the turn Bradley.

She practically tiptoed to keep the heels from adding to the soundtrack. She was listening for something—anything. But there was nothing. No sounds, no fighting, no fuss, and no other gunshots—that is, not until she was just about at the corner.

Sandy could hear Bradley say, "What the fuck?"

Worried that something had happened to him, she ceased moving cautiously, picked up speed, and darted around the corner to stand next to him. In fact, she had nearly run to that spot where he stood in the middle of the sidewalk, one hand on his hip and the other hand holding his service weapon at his side.

She joined him in looking down over a body that was sprawled on the ground. The body lay flat on its back, its arms and head on the sidewalk, with its legs lying mostly in the street. It looked as if someone had carelessly thrown this body—and it had landed in the wrong place. There was a huge, gaping hole over what had been the heart.

"Gurganus," Sandy said in a whisper.

"Get back! You don't know if the shooter is still here," Bradley directed.

Sandy didn't hear him. She stared at Gurganus. She was amazed—astonished, really. Then she saw him move.

It was the slightest twitch of his hand. She watched it. She knew that hand, with the same black, wiry hairs on the knuckles she had encountered years ago. That hand had tortured her. It had tortured her once while she was awake, but hundreds of times while she dreamt. She could feel her face redden at the memory of that hand.

The memory made her eyes immediately look at his face. His eyes were staring at her. His lips—were they moving?

Bradley grabbed her arm. It wasn't a forceful grab, but the kind that a man does when he grabs a ladies arm to lead her into a doorway. Still, Sandy didn't move.

"He's alive," Sandy said in disbelief.

Sandy pulled away from Bradley and knelt by Gurganus's head. Bradley initially tried to hold her back, but he realized soon thereafter that it was futile. Truth be told, he didn't know what to do. Was this her chance for closure, or was this making it worse?

Sandy watched as Gurganus's lips tried to move again. He was trying to whisper something to her. She leaned in, close enough that his lips nearly touched her ear. Immediately, she smelled the stench of his cigarettes.

She strained to hear his one word: "Help."

She pulled back as if she had been bitten. She looked at Bradley. "He said help." She couldn't believe it. Somewhere deep inside, she had expected him to say that he was sorry or to acknowledge who she was or to confess to his crimes. Something. But *help*?

"Me help you?" she said to him. She was shocked. She stood up, unable to get to her feet quickly enough. It was as if she was afraid he would touch her again.

"*Me help you?!*" she yelled down at him.

In the distance, she heard an officer yelling out to Bradley and then heard Bradley telling the officer to call an ambulance. She heard him say that, yes, he and Sandy were okay.

Gurganus's eyes looked confused.

"Even now, this son of a bitch doesn't realize who I am," she said to no one in particular.

Sandy kicked him in the side. Hard. "Remember me now, you son of a bitch?"

His eyebrows arched inward, showing his utter confusion. She could hear the soft gurgling noise from inside his body as his lungs filled with his own blood. Sandy grimaced.

She had dreamt of choking the life out of him, but now, actually seeing and hearing his body manifest her dream made her head swim. She was growing nauseous. But her hatred stole away every bit of compassion she might have otherwise shown. She stepped toward him again.

Bradley pulled her back.

"Sandy," he began.

She pulled away from Curtis, not even looking at him, and bent over Gurganus. She began shoving at him. "Remember me now?" she yelled at him. Her shoves turned into slaps and punches. She knelt on one knee, wanting to strike out, wanting to hurt him, but inflicting pain only on herself.

Gurganus's body began to twitch with the unintended motions a body makes as its last-ditch effort to cling to life. His breathing became even more strained as his lungs now virtually had no room into which to pull air. Blood began to pour out of his mouth in one long, thick stream. Sandy watched in horror as it bubbled out slowly.

And then nothing.

Sandy pulled her hands back close to her chest. She stared at him.

"He's dead, Sandy. He's dead. Stop!" Bradley pulled her up.

Another officer had made his way from the jail. He had made it just to the parking lot before yelling out, "What the fuck, Curtis?"

Bradley thought fast. "It's just one of our ADAs. She was doing chest compressions. I think he's gone already. Call the paramedics."

The officer met Bradley's response with an odd expression on his face. But it seemed to be an acceptable response, as he simply turned back around, walked to a nearby police car, and reached into it to radio for help.

Sandy stared at Gurganus. Gurganus's eyes stared back. They were empty eyes that had been cold long before his death had turned them that way.

Bradley turned Sandy to face him. He held her shoulders tight and forced her to look him in the eyes.

"Sandy, I want you to walk to your car now. Listen to me. I want you to walk to your car now. Get in your car and drive. Drive all the way to the cabin. Don't think about it. Don't argue. Just go. Do you understand me?"

Sandy looked back at Gurganus. Bradley forcefully yanked her back. Their eyes met.

"Sandy, this is not a game. You must go—and you must go now."

Sandy seemed to really look at him this time. "Okay," she said. "But what about …"

Bradley interrupted her. "Sandy, go to your car. Get home to the cabin. Go now!"

Sandy didn't argue. She did as he demanded. And she didn't look back.

CHAPTER 19

SHE COULDN'T TELL YOU ONE THING ABOUT THE DRIVE FROM THE heart of New Orleans to her family's Arcadian cabin. Not one word. Did she take her normal route? Did she speed? Was the city traffic unusually busy as everyone made an escape from the storm? Did she stop to get gas? Who knew? Truthfully, who cared?

At some point in time, she became present. She turned onto the curving driveway, saw the wide-open lawn in front of the cabin, and was suddenly plucked from dreamland and dropped into the front seat of her sassy little car. She didn't feel sassy, though. In fact, she didn't feel much of anything. She had no thoughts, no concerns—just a heavy mind riding in the front seat with her.

She parked on the side of the cabin and looked around for whatever it was she was going to take inside with her. Her purse? Her overnight bag?

But there was nothing there. It dawned on her that she didn't have a single thing with her. She shrugged at herself, turned the ignition off, and climbed out of the car to make the short walk to the back door.

She quickened her step. In fact, she rushed to the back of the cabin and fumbled to get her key into the door before finally making her way inside. Sandy slammed the door behind herself and then leaned with her back against it.

Slowly, she slid down onto the floor. As she did so, Sandy pulled her knees tight against her chest and braced her body with her arms. It was as if she feared she'd go straight through the wooden planks. Her head was swimming.

She looked down at the edge of her skirt, noticing for the first time the small spots of blood from the man who had abused her when she was eight. Then the tears came, expressing years of tucked-away anger, her anxiety about the trial, and her fear that he would get away with it.

It all came to a boiling point right then and there, behind the back door, on the floor of the cabin. She couldn't hold it back any longer. Her tears turned to sobs; she struggled to keep her breath. Her eyes never left her bloodstained skirt. The blood … she remembered his blood coming down the side of his mouth in that thick, warm stream and his eyes pleading with her for help.

Sandy was exhausted. She was spent. She covered her eyes. She begged her God, "Why me?" And she wept. Her self-pity made her even angrier as she cursed herself for feeling this way. *Why not me? Why* not *me?* she thought, blaming herself for what Gurganus had done to her, as if it were a punishment for each stupid thing she had done in her life.

She said out loud to no one but herself, "You deserved it." Then she wiped her tears, knowing deep down that this wasn't true. She sat there for several moments catching her breath. Then she realized that her hand had landed on her skirt edge. She was touching his blood!

In sheer panic, she pulled herself up and began pulling at her clothing. She needed the clothes to come off. She needed them off now! This instant!

She tore at her wet jacket. There was no space for anything else in her mind other than getting those clothes off of her body.

She wanted his blood gone once and for all. The belt on her jacket was double-knotted; she frantically pulled at it. She had to get it off—and she had to get it off right now! Finally freeing herself of the belt, she pulled at the only two buttons that remained buttoned. As she loosened the second one, the belt strap in her hand fell to the floor. As she bent to grab the belt, her eyes noticed something odd. It stopped her in her tracks.

Sandy saw, just barely poking out from the underside of the couch, her dad's brown leather shoes. She didn't much consider why she thought it to be so odd, but she had noticed something peculiar about the way the shoes looked. Her dad was meticulous. He never left his shoes out, much less tucked them away under the couch.

She moved a little closer, having altogether forgotten that she had been trying to rid herself of that jacket and that she had dropped the belt.

Then it dawned on her: the shoes were various shades of brown. Most of the shoes' surface had been darkened by water. She bent down to touch them, feeling the cold leather underneath her hands. They were still damp. She could see the edge of the floor vent, which is when she realized that the shoes had been placed there to dry. Why to dry?

Sandy listened carefully for any evidence of her father's presence in the cabin. She could hear the shower running, faintly.

Sandy stood and, without giving it much thought, began slowly making her way to her father's bedroom. The sound of the shower grew stronger as she rounded the corner. What did she expect to find? Why this inexplicable feeling of dread in the pit of her stomach?

The bedroom was dark, with the exception of her dad's nightstand lamp, which he had flipped on and which bathed the room in a warm glow. Across the armchair next to his nightstand, Sandy saw her father's gray suit, the one he had been wearing that day. She enjoyed a brief feeling of relief, knowing that it was definitely him who was in the shower.

Sandy walked toward the suit. Picking it up, she felt the cold, wet material under her hand. *What? Why so wet?* She held the suit close to her chest, trying to make sense of the situation.

She couldn't explain exactly what was so confusing to her, but something just wasn't right. Behind her, the shower stopped. Moments later, she heard the shower curtain slide open.

She took a seat in his chair and laid her father's suit across her lap. Within minutes, her father appeared in the bathroom doorway. Dressed in sweatpants and a T-shirt, he looked just like he did when at the cabin—except for his face.

Once he saw Sandy sitting there in his room, his face turned white, as if he had seen a ghost.

"Dad?" she began to question. Her face was soft; her eyebrows were arched in confusion.

"No. Don't."

Sandy slightly lifted her father's suit, her head cocked to the side, questioning.

He sighed. His expression was one of hurt and distance as he said, "I'm not doing this. You have no right to ask."

Sandy pulled the wet jacket to her chest. She instantly knew; she instantly put it all together. "How did you know? When did you ..." She stopped. She wasn't quite sure what she even wanted to ask.

"Sandy, you didn't really think I could ever forget his name, did you? That night, that night I helped you prepare for the motions hearing, I knew the instant I saw his name. I vowed that this case would mark the last time that I—or you—ever saw it."

Sandy's face couldn't hide her shock. Her eyebrows raised and her mouth dropped open. She stared blankly at her father. He looked away, his eyes burning holes into the floor.

"But," she began.

He quickly held up his hand, stopping her. He said firmly, "Don't ever ask me to tell you the truth." His eyes began to well up with tears.

Sandy stared at her father as if for the first time in her life. It dawned on her that that beast of a man, Gurganus, had claimed her father's life, too. That beast of a man had haunted her father's dreams, too. That beast of a man was what monsters were made of, to both of them.

Tears began to fall slowly and silently down her father's face. Sandy thought about all those years when she asked herself why her. She realized that her dad asked why, too. She thought about all those years when she had blamed herself. She realized that her dad had blamed himself, too.

The fact that her father was hurting just as much as she was made her feel better in that she was not alone—and also worse, in that she was not alone, because the man she loved the most was the one next to her. So many years had passed and no one spoke of it—no one spoke of him. All these years, the Morgans had all pretended that it hadn't happened.

Sandy nodded slightly. Her father nodded back. It was as if they both acknowledged a silent agreement: whatever happened tonight would forever remain unspoken.

Sandy's father walked toward her, took the jacket from her hand, and threw it carelessly on the floor. Then, taking her hand, he pulled her up toward him.

Putting his hands on her shoulders, he looked her in the eyes. In a voice little more than a whisper, he said, "Sometimes a father has secrets that only he is strong enough to bear. They are the type of secrets that a father takes to his grave. This is my cross to bear—mine alone. But I want you to know that I was never going to let him hurt you again, even if this time it was just in the courtroom."

Sandy choked on her words, fighting back tears, as she said, "But what about you?"

Her father took her right hand and placed it over his heart. "This heart is a rock. I can take hit after hit and face whatever comes. If my whole world faded and was gone, as long as I have you and your mother, I am not afraid."

Sandy saw what she thought was a flash of anger in his eyes when he looked away and said, "I was there the moment you were born, and I can tell you that you were born into love. For that love, I would trade my freedom. I would trade my life. I won't apologize for that."

His face softened as he glanced at her face. He looked away again before continuing. "I suppose I never forgave myself for what happened to you. It was my job to protect you, and I didn't."

"Dad," Sandy began to protest, grabbing his hands in hers.

But her father shook his head and then looked her in the eye. He said, "I'll never forgive myself for being a failure when you needed me most. All those years that passed, that you seemed to forget— maybe I just prayed that you had. When I saw your file and watched you struggle just to read it, I knew he was back—back to make you remember the worst day of your life. I wanted you to have justice your way. Sometimes, though, you can't find true justice in a courtroom. But maybe now some of the wrong I did in not protecting my eight- year-old daughter has been made right."

Her father dropped his hands and then his eyes. Shrugging, he said, "Maybe I made it worse. Maybe when he burns in hell, so will our feelings about him. Or, maybe when he burns in hell, so will our memories of him. What I know for certain is that I'll be here with you when it's all over. I'll be here for you this time. I'll trade my place in heaven to make this right for you. Only for you. My little girl, I'd do it for you."

Her father's tears fell freely now, as did her own. She reached out and hugged him, suddenly eight again, with her daddy there to catch her just as she was about to fall into a dark abyss. They cried together. He petted the back of her hair as she rested her head on his chest.

Suddenly, their heads jerked toward the door once they heard Sandy's mother's singsong voice call out from the living room. "It's just me, guys!"

They looked at each other again. Sandy's father said in a whisper, "We will never speak of this again." They both wiped their faces and struggled to resume normal breathing over their sobs.

Sandy put on her serious lawyer face and asked, "Speak of what?"

Her father gave her a small but soft smile. "That's my girl," he said as he wrapped his arms around her. They hugged.

Sandy's mother appeared in the doorway and stopped in her tracks at the sight of them. "What's wrong?" Her eyebrows were crossed in fear.

Her father cleared his throat. His voice returned to express his normal, although less than jolly, self. "Oh, just proud of our little girl here!"

Sandy's mother clasped her hands together just under her chin as she said excitedly, "Oh, your case! How did it go?"

Sandy looked at her dad, then back at her mom, and smiled. "I guess you could say I won."

CHAPTER 20

It ended up being a late night for both Sandy and her father. Sandy, who couldn't sleep, kept thinking about the brown box that was waiting in her trunk. *Why had I brought him here with me?* she asked herself over and over again. *Why?*

She crept out of the cabin to her car and opened the trunk. In the darkness, her trunk light shone onto the small brown box. *Now what the hell am I going to do with this?* she thought. It occurred to her just then what to do! She ran back into the house and then back to her trunk to retrieve the box.

She made her way to the trash burn pile, brown box and lighter in hand. Sandy removed the file from the box. Then she placed the brown box into the trash barrel and flicked the lighter on. She tried a couple of tries before the orange danced, bright against her hand. She moved the flame to the corner of the box and watched it slowly ignite. She stared wide-eyed as the fire expanded to engulf most of the box.

She opened the file and turned to the first page. Not bothering to unclasp it, she ripped it from file. She slowly put a corner of the paper into the fire, letting it catch. She ripped out the next page and again placed one corner of paper in the fire, watching it burn before dropping it into the burn pile. Then she proceeded to do the same thing with each and every page thereafter. There were over three hundred of them.

One by one, she destroyed each page—and she thought of her own childhood. She recalled her own little voice testifying. She recalled the words he had spoken to her as he hurt her. She recalled his face as blood dripped from his mouth and he pled for her help. She could almost hear his lungs pushing and pulling for his final breaths. Her tears fell freely as she remembered Dori and thought about all the other countless little girls who were hurt by him and others like him. She thought of how afraid he must have been as he made his journey to hell after dying alone outside a jailhouse on the streets of New Orleans. She thought that she should be, in some small way, thankful not to have been a victim, but to have been a survivor—about how every little thing in her life, the good and the bad, had led her to experience this exact moment of clarity. She thought that Gurganus's violence against her hadn't defined her before and wouldn't define her now. It was part of her—but it wasn't all of her.

There were fewer than a dozen pages left when she realized that he was standing behind her. He was crying, too, although silently. He was there for her even now, when she wasn't aware of his presence. He didn't say a word. She smiled at him—not a happy smile, but a smile of thanks and sadness. He nodded at her. She threw the last page into the fire and hugged the now empty file folder close. She stared at the flame and at the little bits of ash that drifted here and there on the wind.

Finally, she pulled the file away from her chest and gave it a good look. The designation *State of Louisiana v. Bruce Gurganus* still shone, even in the darkness. She said a silent prayer for the little girl she used to be and asked God to let that little girl heal and go in peace. She prayed for her father and for God to forgive and protect him. Then she tossed the file folder into the fire. She watched it curl and crackle as the fire's oranges and reds consumed it.

She felt his arms wrap around her from behind. They stood together with the flames lighting their faces softly. Whatever the burning of those pages meant to each of them was personal, and neither would discuss it. The brown box was gone now, gone forever, leaving only a silent understanding between a father and a daughter.

As the flame burned out, he took her hand and led her back to the cabin. Silently, they went home—together. Making it to her bedroom, she turned to find her father standing in his bedroom doorway across from hers. She said softly, "Good night, Dad."

"Good night, doll."

They both slept with their doors open.

CHAPTER 21

SANDY SAT QUIETLY ON THE FRONT PORCH SWING. STILL IN HER pajamas, she had one leg lying across the swing and the other dangling and haphazardly touching the porch, which allowed her to give the occasional push. The chains of the porch swing creaked. A gentle breeze blew, occasionally touching her face and playing along the free curls that had loosened from her ponytail in her sleep.

Her mother, Rose, gently rocked in her rocking chair at the center of the porch, near the door. She worked carefully on a cross-stitch, silently pulling and pushing the colorful thread into and out of the fabric.

Sandy watched her mom for a moment. It briefly crossed her mind that it was nice seeing her sitting there, comfortably rocking. Then it unexpectedly dawned on Sandy that this was what her mother had always been. She was quiet and lovely, always in the background, unassuming and humble. Her mom was the first to offer help. She was a gentle and kind woman. Sandy knew instantly that she and her father couldn't be who they were without her mother behind them both. Rose, in many ways, was their rock.

Sandy smiled at her mother, who hadn't noticed that she had held Sandy's attention for so long. Turning her attention back to the swaying Spanish moss hanging from the cypress trees, Sandy took a deep breath of humid country air.

Sandy always loved sitting on this porch on the day after a storm. The rains usually passed to leave behind an overcast and windy day. The weather wasn't so nice that it guilted a person into actually going out and doing something, but it was nice enough that one felt comfortable sitting outside and enjoying the wind. Had the day before not been what it was, then this would have been just another lazy Saturday morning.

The screen door creaked open. Within moments, Sandy's father appeared. Tucked under his arm was the newspaper, which he always read first thing in the morning. He walked without comment to the porch swing, lifted up Sandy's leg, sat down next to her, and then placed her leg in his lap.

As he began to unfold the paper, Rose put her cross-stitch in her lap and said, "I made coffee, Thomas, want me to fix you a cup?"

"No, doll. Not right now," he said, giving her the special smile and wink he reserved for her alone. She smiled back and resumed rocking.

"So, forget to set your alarm clock?" Sandy asked.

"Cute," her father said. "I don't believe I've slept this late in years."

"I slept like a rock, too," Sandy said absently.

"Oh, I didn't say I slept well, I just slept late," he said, devoid of any emotion.

Sandy smiled and nodded at him.

They sat this way for a long while, the only sound coming from the wind as it occasionally wrestled her father's newspaper.

Sandy jumped up and pointed. "Look!" she exclaimed.

Rose dropped her cross-stitch. Her father crumbled the paper in his lap, trying to get a glimpse.

"Look! Right there!" Sandy said. She was pointing at a large, wet bullfrog that had jumped to the top of the steps.

"I can't believe it!" she went on. "All these years, and finally I see one! Sitting right there, as if he's making fun of me."

Rose gave a small giggle and went back to her cross-stitch. Her father barely even glanced at the frog before saying, "Uh-huh, told you so. Right before your eyes."

171

Sandy swore that the bullfrog was looking right at her, almost teasing her. He croaked deeply a few times before jumping off into the green grass.

Sandy's eyes followed him even after he was long gone. For a brief moment, everything seemed to make sense to her. Everything seemed to have come full circle. Everything seemed right.

"You know, Dad, I've been thinking." Sandy leaned back on the porch swing, pulling her knees up to her chest and hugging them to her body.

"Dangerous sport, my dear," he responded dryly, not even looking her way.

Sandy reached across to her father and gently took the newspaper out of his hands. She folded it neatly, put it in her lap, and then turned to look at him.

"Oh, I see," he said, "this is the part where you insist on sharing what you are thinking!" He leaned back as if to get comfortable, and then he said theatrically, "Please, indulge us."

Then he couldn't help but grin. Hell, he even broke a smile and paid full attention to his daughter as if awaiting some big news.

"Well, it just sort of occurred to me that maybe you need a criminal division at your office."

Silence.

Her father couldn't hide his surprise. His gasp was small but audible.

"Criminal division?" he asked tentatively. His voice asked if he had understood her correctly, but his eyes told a different story, one of surprise, excitement, and disbelief. "I'm listening," he said cautiously.

"You know, Dad," Sandy continued, shrugging her shoulders as if her suggestion was a brilliant one, "a seasoned prosecutor would make a great addition to the office. Someone who knows all the ins and outs of the criminal courts could be a huge asset."

He continued to look at her in disbelief, which eventually changed into something else. Was it pride? Excitement? Damn, she still couldn't read him.

Then Sandy reached across and put the newspaper back in her father's lap. He unfolded it, leaned back, and began to pretend to read it as he said, "Well, I'm not so sure we are still hiring."

Sandy smiled and leaned her back against the arm rail, placing her feet back into her father's lap. "Fine, I'm sure there are several other civil law firms that would be happy to have me," she said, her tone feigning unconcern. *Two can play his game,* she thought. "Or maybe I just go out on my own and become your fiercest competition."

Her father couldn't contain himself. He rolled up the newspaper and begin swatting at her while he said, "My competition! I bet! You're hired! Now, give me a hug. By the way, it's about time!"

In the midst of his hugging her and tearing his newspaper in the process, Rose jumped onto both of their laps. The porch swing creaked in protest. There were tears enough for everyone.

The family's chatter quickly turned to Sandy's giving her two-week notice at the district attorney's office; which office would be hers in her father's large downtown firm; how her father mustn't remind her about taking her vitamins while she was at work; and other exciting plans.

"Just imagine it," Sandy said, "Morgan and Morgan, law partners!"

Her father feigned objecting as he said, "Partners? You are lucky I am hiring you back!"

After a while, Rose got up from the rocking chair to go inside and see about breakfast. As she stood, something grabbed her attention. She pointed to the end of the drive. "And who could that be?" she asked.

Sandy's father strained his eyes to see. A black truck turns into the long winding driveway. Recognizing the truck, he said, "Oh, that is just Sandy's friend." He made air quotes as he said the word *friend.*

Sandy let out a breath that she hadn't even realized she was holding. She smiled at her mom. "Yes, Mom, that's my friend, all right."

ARITA M. L. BOHANNAN

In her rush, Sandy made it into the house before her mother did, yelling over her shoulder, "entertain him for a minute while I get dressed."

Rose looked at her husband with an eyebrow raised. He smiled, shrugged his shoulders, and stood to greet Detective Curtis as he finally reached the side of the house to park, and said, "In her defense, he is obviously a very special friend."

Detective Curtis spent the evening with the Morgans. As they sat around the table after dinner, sharing a bottle of wine, he filled them in on the investigation into Gurganus's death. He explained that the circumstances were bizarre in that the only suspect was Lee Lawson. Everyone knew he hated Gurganus. He had even tried to attack him in the courtroom in front of a dozen witnesses, including the judge. But Mr. Lawson, having been informed that Gurganus was murdered, had promptly gone to the police station to give a statement.

Curtis continued. "So, Lawson was at a well-known local restaurant with the Dauzats when Gurganus was shot. When I asked him if he had anything to do with the murder, he actually looked sad when he said, 'I wish!' That guy has some guts. I mean, I believe him. I think he wished he had killed him." Curtis went on to say that Lawson's alibi checked out and that he was quickly ruled out as a suspect.

"So, what now?" Rose asked, fascinated that this had all happened in one of her daughter's cases—and completely clueless that it directly affected her own life.

"You know, sometimes these things just go without being solved or without the police ever finding out who did it," Bradley explained, shrugging. "Quite frankly," he continued, "I don't think any of us in the department are going to waste a lot of time trying to figure it out. Sometimes these assholes simply get what they have coming to them."

Curtis reached across the table and gave Sandy's hand a squeeze. He was thinking, *Thank God I stopped her from pulling the trigger.*

Sandy was thinking, *Yes. This asshole just got what he had coming to him.*

CPSIA information can be obtained at www.ICGtesting.com
Printed in the USA
LVOW08s0417310114

371693LV00002B/91/P